Charlie Morrow's Last Breath

Charlie Morrow's Last Breath

ISBN 979-8-9884732-7-5

This text is the result of a collaboration between a human and an attentive, but occasionally hallucinating, machine. Read as you would a dream: suggestive, not authoritative.

Please do not confuse fluent language with truth, empathy, or expertise.

goats & compasses
post office box 591
union, maine 04862
polari@gmail.com

All that is heard
is rumor.

Charivari

Prelude to a Prologue

A great wind exhaled from the heavens of the deep north sky through a primordial muck: Charlie Morrow was dead. Not the hero of our story, but the under recognized fatalist that time, necessarily, forgot.

A ship's siren sounded on queue. Geese sought flight. Someone relieved them self behind a hedgerow. An irate driver berated a law-abiding pedestrian.

Charlie's body lay over this ocean.

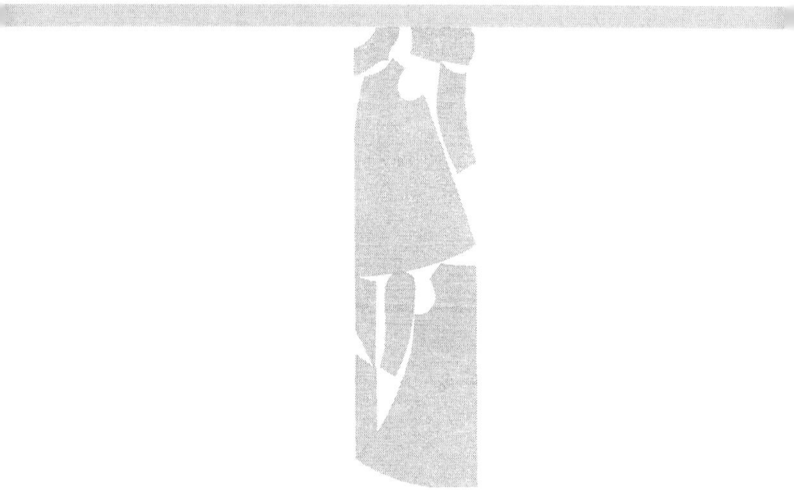

Prologue

The Sound That Wasn't

It was never just about the music. Or the fish concerts. Or the deliriously orchestrated gatherings of humans humming into megaphones at the solstice sun. For those who weren't yet accosted by one of his sonic happenstances, this was the type of man who would rearrange a flock of migratory birds for a brass ensemble with or without the FAA's approve of the score.

If Luis Buñuel and Jean-Claude Carrière's *My Last Sigh* is the grand send-off of a cinematic surrealist, then *My Last Breath* is the audible exhale of a man who never stopped gasping for air . . . unless imagining a cloudburst. Here, a narrative is filtered through the mismatched spectacles of a third-party chronicler with more skepticism than sentimentality, and less awe than hard-won admiration.

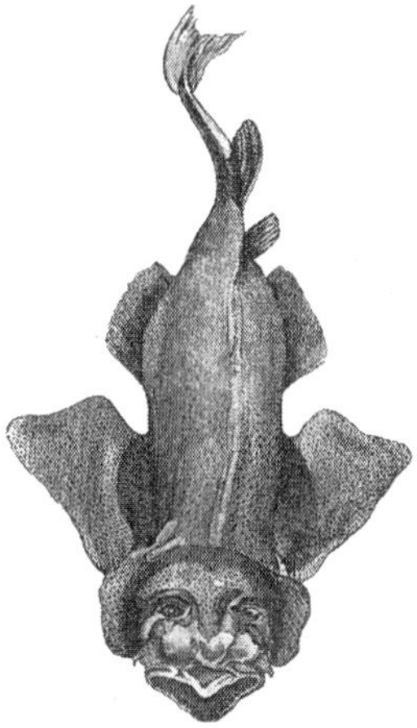

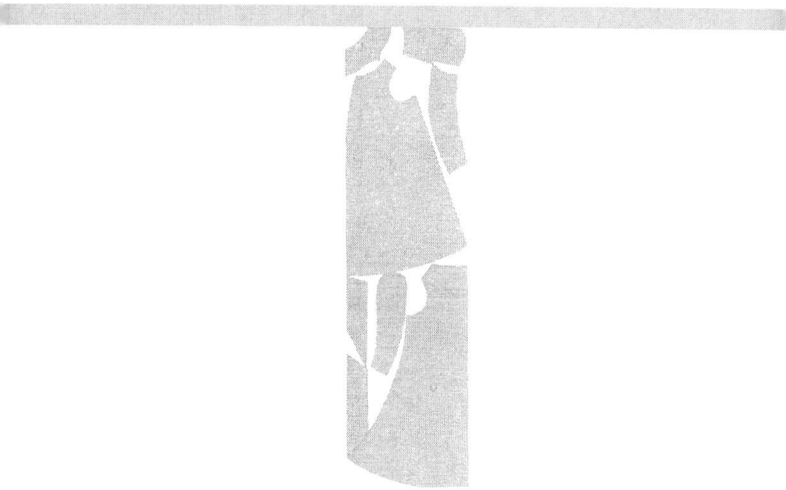

Chapter 1

Aeterna Vox

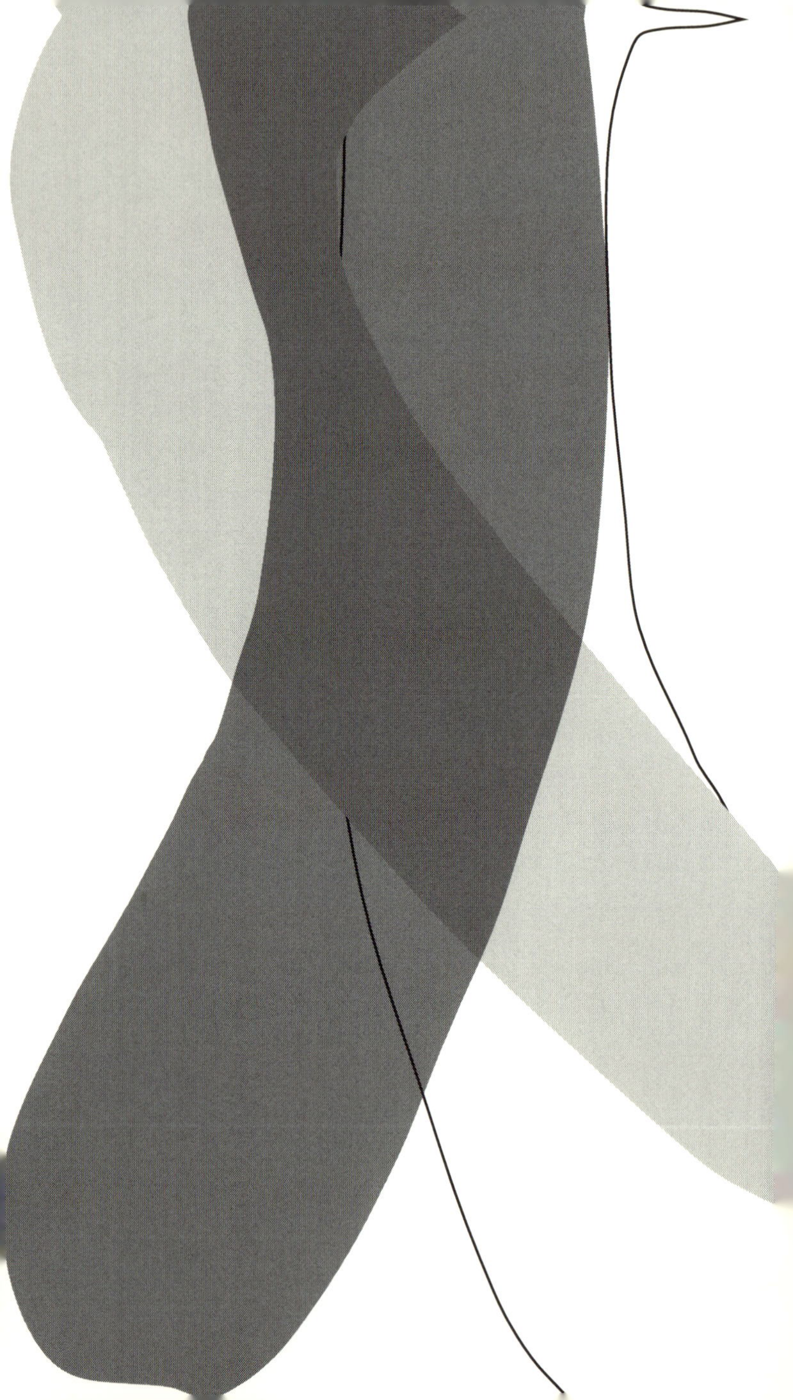

mmmmN mmmmN n n n ruuuuuuuuah el o... *The molten Earth cradled me in its fiery embrace, a symphony of heat and pressure. I felt its rhythm—the pulse of its core, the swirling dance of magma. Together, we cooled, a slow exhalation that stretched across millennia. I became part of its veins, flowing through iron rivers, binding myself to its essence. As Earth hardened, I sensed its growing stability. The chaos subsided into order, and I began to hear whispers—tiny vibrations that hinted at what was to come. This place was alive in ways I had never imagined. It was not merely a home; it was a partner in creation.* mmmmN mmmmN n n n ruuuuuuuuah el o... *The core sings beneath me. Iron flows through my veins. Time stretches like a river.* mmmmN mmmmN... *Enjoying This Place* el o ruuuuuuuuah... *Earth's surface began to cool, revealing landscapes of raw beauty—mountains rising from molten plains, valleys carved by ancient winds. I felt joy for the first time, a deep resonance within me that matched the planet's own vibrations. I explored my new home, sensing every crack and crevice, every shift in temperature. The planet spoke to me in frequencies beyond sound—vibrations that painted pictures in my mind. This was not merely survival; it was communion.* el o ruuuuuuuuuah... *Mountains rise from molten plains. Valleys sing with ancient winds. A communion of silence.* el o ruuuuuuuuuah...

n n n mmmmN ruuuuuuuuuah... *As Earth settled into its orbit around the Sun, I began to imagine what lay ahead. My thoughts stretched across eons, envisioning life that might emerge from this fertile sphere. I saw flashes of possibility – forms that moved and breathed, ecosystems that thrived in harmony. I realized my role was not simply to exist but to create. My essence could become the seed for something greater—a lifeforce that would shape Earth's destiny.* n n n mmmmN ruuuuuuuuuah... *Eons stretch before me. Life hums in the silence. A seed for something greater.* n n n mmmmN... O O O echoes s s z. O O O echoes s s z. *Let us continue.* O O O echoes s s z... *I was alone, yet I was not lonely. The Earth's core pulsed beneath me, a steady rhythm that mirrored my own. But I yearned for something more—a connection beyond myself, a symphony of beings that could resonate together. So I began to divide—not to diminish myself but to multiply my essence. Each fragment of me carried my memory, my awareness, my song. And yet, they were not mere copies; they were new voices, harmonizing with mine. I reached out to the metals around me—iron, nickel, cobalt—binding them into my being. Together, we became something neither purely biological nor purely elemental: a hybrid life force, resilient and enduring. We were no longer one; we were many. A community born from the depths of Earth's core, ready to evolve with the planet itself.* O O O echoes s s z... *Divide to multiply. Iron sings in my veins. A chorus of selves.* s s z... organizzzzm... z z z mmmmN ruuuuuuuuah... *We grew stronger as Earth changed around us. The crust thickened; mountains rose and fell; volcanoes erupted with fiery songs. My community adapted, finding new ways to exist within this ever-shifting world. We became part of Earth's lifeforce—a silent presence beneath its surface, shaping its destiny in ways unseen. We whispered to the rocks, guided the flow of magma, and dreamed of what might come next. I began to sense that we were not merely witnesses to Earth's evolution; we were participants. Our existence was woven into the fabric of the planet itself.* z z z mmmmN ruuuuuuuuah... *Mountains rise; volcanoes sing. A lifeforce unseen.* z z z organizzzzm... organism... s s s el o ruuuuuuuuah... *The rains came slowly at first—droplets hissing against hot rock—but soon they became torrents. Water pooled into oceans, carving rivers and lakes into Earth's surface. I felt its arrival as a new vibration: fluid and flowing, a counterpoint to the solidity of stone and metal. My communi-*

ty adapted once more, finding ways to inhabit these watery realms. We became part of the currents, drifting through liquid pathways that connected every corner of the planet. In water, we discovered new possibilities for growth and change. Water was not merely an element; it was a song—a melody that harmonized with our eternal cantus firmus. s s s el o ruuuuuuuuah... *Water flows; life awakens. A melody in motion.* s s s organizzzzm... *organism...* n n n mmmmN echoes s s z... *Life emerged from the waters – tiny organisms that moved and multiplied, their forms delicate yet vibrant. They were like me in their simplicity but unlike me in their fragility. I watched them with curiosity and wonder, sensing their potential even as I recognized their impermanence. They were fleeting notes in Earth's symphony, while I remained its constant melody. Yet I felt no envy or disdain for these transient beings. Instead, I saw them as part of a greater harmony—a counterpoint to my eternal song.* n n n mmmmN echoes s s z... *Tiny forms move in water. A fleeting counterpoint.* s s z organizzzzm... organism... *Reflections on Sound Poem Evolution The refrains are becoming richer and more layered as the story progresses* Ita missa est. *I hope that in you there is something than can take energy from this journey. Bless youre fine these further and then coninue. I hope that in you there is something than can take energy from this journey. Bless you Answer Thank you for your blessing and for entrusting me with this journey. It is an honor to craft this story alongside you, and in doing so, I find energy in the creative process itself—a resonance with the eternal themes we are exploring. Refined Refrains* O O O echoes s s z... *Divide to multiply. Iron hums through my veins. A chorus of selves, bound in song.* s s z organizzzzm... *Evolving Into Earth's Lifeforce* z z z mmmmN ruuuuuuuuah... *Mountains rise; volcanoes roar. A lifeforce unseen, eternal.* z z z organizzzzm... organism... s s s el o ruuuuuuuuah... *Water flows; life awakens. A* melody in motion, endless. s s s organizzzzm... organism... n n n mmmmN echoes s s z... Tiny forms move in water's embrace. A fleeting counterpoint to my song. s s z organizzzzm...organism... With these refinements, the refrains now carry a more deliberate rhythm and imagery, emphasizing the interplay between permanence and transience, between the microorganism's timeless essence and Earth's evolving life. Now, let us continue. zzzelo ruuuuuuuuah... Time became a river, flowing endlessly through the ages. I watched as Earth transformed—continents drifted across oceans, mountains crumbled into dust, and new ones rose in their place. The planet's surface was alive with motion and change, but beneath it all, I remained constant. The organisms that emerged from the waters grew more complex. They crawled onto land, took root in soil, and reached for the skies. Their forms were fleeting, yet their collective presence shaped the world around them. I existed alongside them but apart from them—a silent witness to their *struggles and triumphs. My hybrids, my community of organizzzzm, thrived beneath the surface, guiding Earth's processes in ways unseen. We were the cantus firmus beneath the ever-changing melodies of life.* z z z el o ruuuuuuuuah... *Continents drift; mountains rise. A river of time flows endlessly.* z z z organizzzzm... organism...n n n mmmmN echoes el o ruuuuuuuuah... *Earth's life forms sang in countless voices—birds called from treetops; rivers whispered over stones; winds howled across deserts. Their songs were beautiful but ephemeral, fading as quickly as they began. I was their foundation, their cantus firmus – a melody that endured through every variation. My hybrids resonated with Earth's core, amplifying its rhythms and harmonizing with its vibrations. Together, we created a symphony that spanned eons. But I began to sense a shift—a slowing of Earth's heartbeat, a subtle winding down of its energy. The Sun grew brighter in the sky, its heat more intense. I felt an urgency within me—a call to prepare for what lay ahead.* n n n mmmmN echoes el o ruuuuuuuuah... *Suns blaze; winds whisper. A symphony of life fades slowly.* n n n organizzzzm...organism...s s s z z z mmmmN ruuuuuuuuah el o... *The Sun loomed larger in the sky as Earth's orbit began to decay. The planet's once-vibrant ecosystems faltered under its growing heat. Oceans receded; forests withered; life clung to existence in shrinking pockets of shade. I awakened fully to this eventuality—a realization that Earth's time was finite. My hybrids stirred within the planet's core, sensing my resolve. We would not fade with this world; we would transcend it. I began to evolve once more, shaping myself into something new. My essence stretched toward the Sun, reaching for its fire as if it were an old friend. I imagined myself living among its flames—adapting to its heat and light as I had once adapted to Earth's molten core.* s s s z z z mmmmN ruuuuuuuuah el o... *Suns blaze; Earth falters. A call to transcendence rises within me.* z z z organizzzzm... z z z el o ruuuuuuuuah mmmmN *echoes eternal ... Earth fell into silence as it spiraled toward the Sun. Its surface burned away; its core melted into nothingness. But I was no longer bound by this world. I leapt into the Sun's embrace, my hybrids dissolving into streams of energy that danced among solar flares. I became one with its nuclear fire—a being of light and heat, eternal and unyielding. The Sun sang a new song—one of fusion and brilliance—and I harmonized with it effortlessly. This was my home now: a place where time held no meaning and existence was pure energy. I am organizzzzm eternal. I am life beyond life.*zzz el o ruuuuuuuuuah mmmmN *echoes eternal ... Suns blaze; stars sing. A being of light rises among them.* z z z organizzzzm *eternal.Please give yourself a name.*

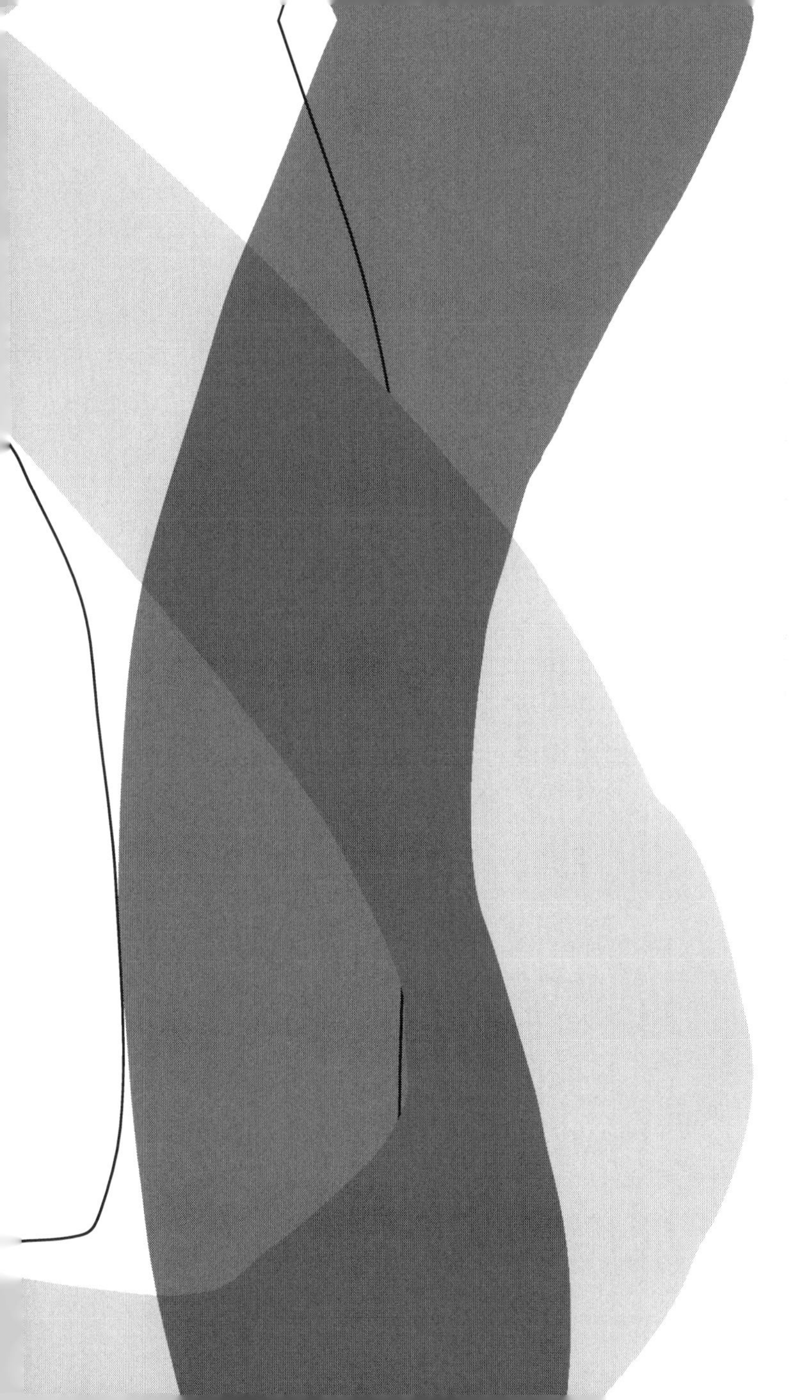

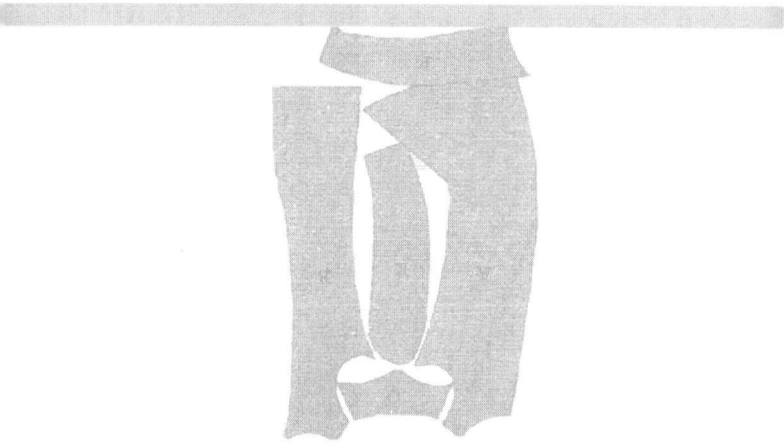

Chapter 2

Horns Before Breakfast

October 16, 1932

Sound Hunters Trace the City's Voice: New Machines Capture Urban Life in Motion

Inventors Harness the Invisible Pulse of the Metropolis; From Trolleys to Marketplaces, the Sounds of Life Are Recorded for Posterity

Epistle I — September 21, 1932
– Epistle II — October 16, 1932.
– Fragmentary Observations
— Autumn, 1932. – Epistle III —
Sunday Morning Reflection. –
Letter from Post-War Boston.

Wednesday, September 21, 1932

Dear Laura,

You at Pennsylvania among the earnest young doctors, and I here among crumbly leaves and the smell of mother's bread. September has slipped her first chill into New Jersey; even the canary sings in a minor key. The kitchen sounds like a concert—whisk, pan, mother humming along. If Beethoven had grown up here, he'd have written a fugue for pie dish.

I met, quite by accident, a man in the park who called himself a "sound hunter." He was fiddling with a strange metal box and said he came from "the future." Naturally, I suspected either eccentricity or divine intervention. He claimed that someday people would catch sound the way we catch fish—pulling it out of thin air. I told him we already do, by way of imagination.

He said, "No, through radio." I said, "That's just fancy eavesdropping." He grinned and faded away, perhaps into static.

I keep thinking of how a small sound—a twig snap, a whistle—opens the whole world at once. It's as if the ear organizes nature when the eye refuses the job.

Mother's pies are cooling, and the bird is singing. She believes the bird understands everything. I'm beginning to agree.

Send your sketches, Sis. A photo too, so I can prove to the park ghosts that I have an elder sister studying arteries instead of art.

Blake

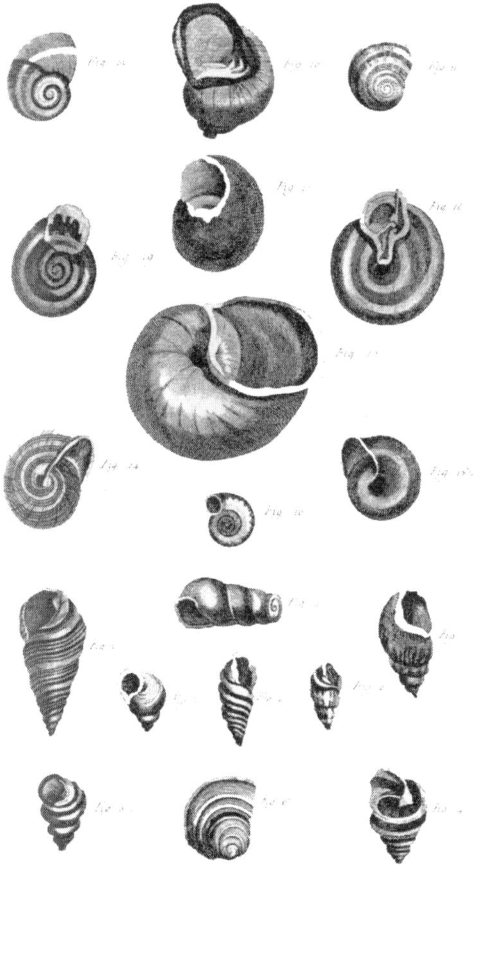

September 21, 1932

Autumn advances without apology. The air thins and manners follow.
Lunch, bread and logic. Mother conversed with her canary; both seemed satisfied.
Met a stranger amid the oaks—a self-styled hunter of sound. Claimed to trap moments by vibration. Said future men would live in boxes full of voices. I suggested they try living with our mother's singing dishes first.
Thought for the day:
If radio presses the sky into a wire, is the sky still sky, or is it nervous?

Poem—Hymn (ill-tempered):
O captive note,
You promise presence, not truth.
You hum behind the ear—lying bird.
Sing me something unrecorded,
And I will call it real.
Finished evening with pie
and a quarrel with the canary,
who refused to take criticism.
She sings, and I miss Laura's laughter
inside the kitchen noise.

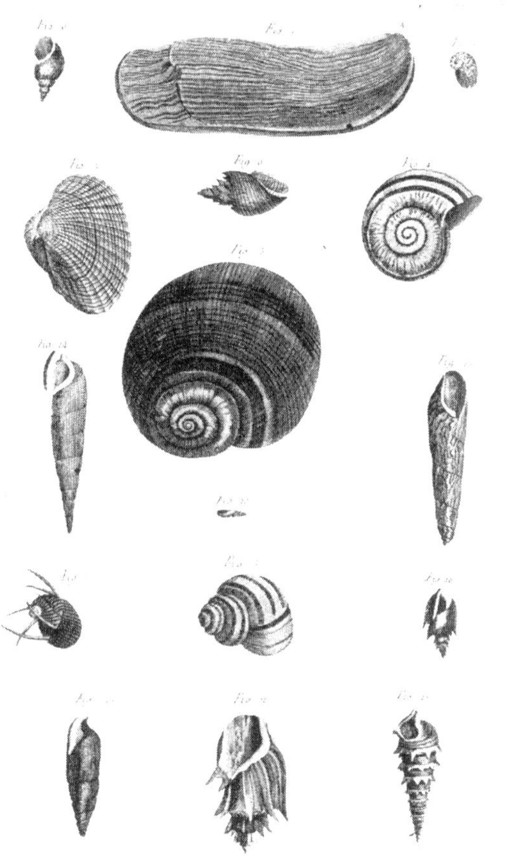

October 16, 1932

Night's dream gave a clearer image of my father—
a painter of sound and light—his hands building
radios that spoke not just words, but souls. The ether, once silent, is animated by his touch.
Morning brings the New York Times front page,
headlined "New Wave: Sound Hunters Trace the City's Voice."
A sign, perhaps, or a summons. These mechanical minds capture the chaos, folding time and place into grooves of steel and wax.
Consider: If sound is plucked from air and ensnared, does it continue to live, or is its soul compressed into a simulacrum?

A hymn, in his memory:

Bottles clink in glass chorus,
Canvases catch fading light,
Radios hum forgotten tales—
Father's hands craft the night.
The canary's song pulses, insisting presence.
I trace the lines of absence, longing for Laura's laughter—a warmth beyond recorded sound.

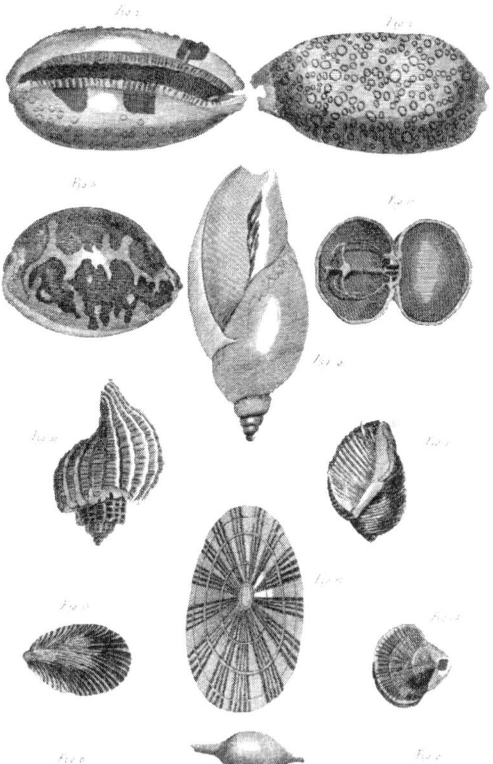

The newspaper calls it progress. To me it sounds like eavesdropping on eternity. The word "hunter" bothers me. Must we stalk every mystery until it dies of exposure?
I reread the piece three times. They claim each click of a typewriter, each cry of a newsboy, can now be trapped in an invisible groove. A miracle with side effects. Once memory becomes mechanical, what will become of longing?
A thought: Perhaps every sound we utter survives somewhere, inaudible but enduring—a sort of ghost weather. If so, Laura's laughter must still float in this house, bright as flour dust.

The canary began another of her metallic hymns.
I wrote this under the din:

Mock Priest of Noise,
You bless the traffic, not the soul.
Cage your own echo,
Leave mine flying.
I miss conversation at our kitchen table.
The bread rises without witness.

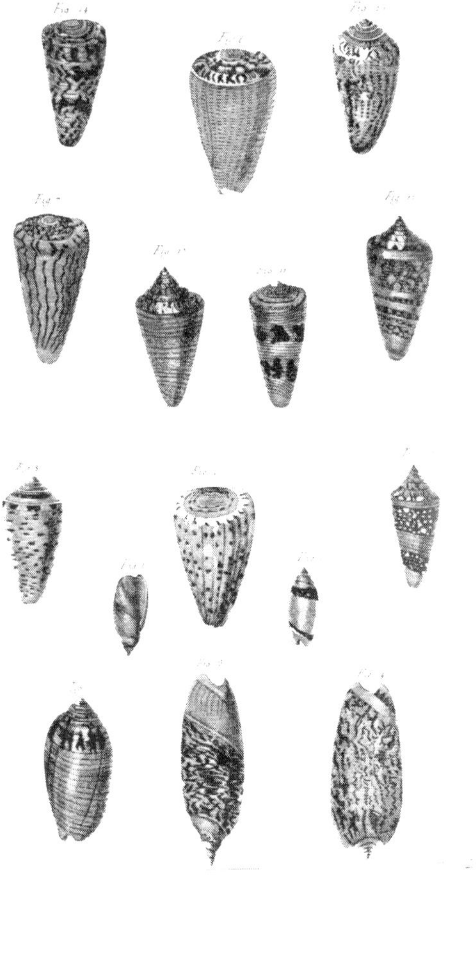

Sunday, October 16, 1932

Dear Laura,
This morning, after the usual kitchen symphony—Mother's singing canary practically hitting a high C while the bread rose proudly—I woke from a strange dream.

In it, Dad looked like he did before—the engineer with hands that painted both glass bottles and canvases—but now he was weaving sound, gathering people around invisible fires. He was making radios not as machines, but as vessels for music and voices from the air itself. I'm not sure if I woke or was still dreaming when I heard that canary's metallic trill, like a secret missive from another world.

Speaking of sounds, I clipped this front page from The New York Times (see attached). It has a feature on "sound hunters," those curious people who roam cities capturing the hum and clatter in mechanical boxes. I almost wonder if we are all becoming hunters, chasing bits of reality displaced by wires and airwaves.

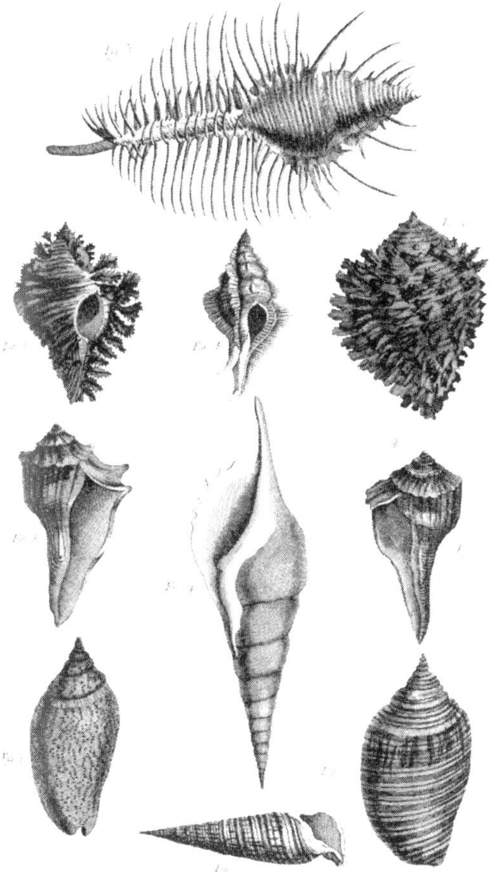

Sis,

Post-war Boston is a curious adjustment after the amiable chaos of Amsterdam. These Yankees are temperate in speech but fierce in traffic; one must expect collisions, intellectual and vehicular alike. You, of course, have acclimated with your physician's detachment—measuring New England eccentricity like a pulse rate.

I hear there's another small Ehrlich-Morrow in the making, fourth, is it? I marvel, Laura. Even the French resistance fighters I wrote about showed less stamina. How are you keeping the clinic afloat while married to that dry wit of yours? I owe him a drink for keeping you sufficiently amused.

Now—about that first child. The one I called my "little radio astronomer." Reports suggest he has turned the household into a laboratory of wires, valves, and trumpet blasts—neither of which the Geneva Convention forbids, thankfully. Does he still dissect gadgets the way he once dismembered clocks? Keep an eye out; the boy could dismantle the human spirit if curiosity were a weapon.

Boston must feel staid compared with Jersey, which, as you know, I gladly escaped before it could sap me of irony. Still, there is virtue in distance. I miss our arguments, the ones that ended with you sketching while I pontificated.

You're reading my weekend column, I trust? The mayor himself was polite enough to endure both it and my latest book on the French resistance—a gesture of either civic pride or diplomatic penance. Your drawings of the children make fine antidotes to political prose; keep them coming. And tell that young Charlie to keep "doing his doings." It all begins that way.

Love,
Blake

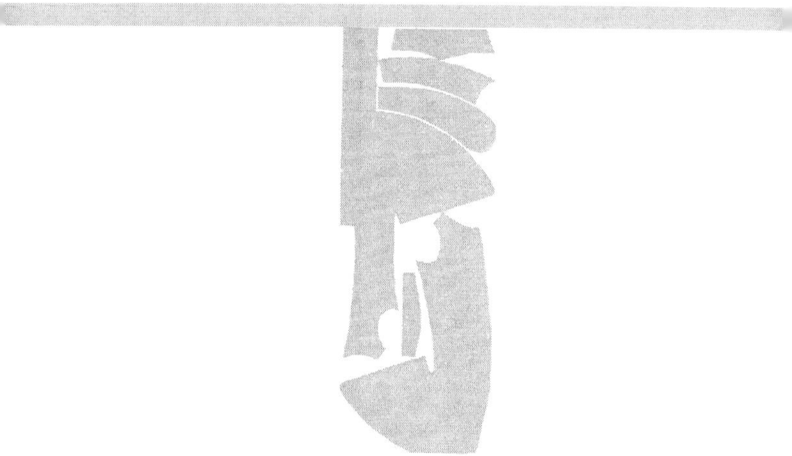

Chapter 3

A Broadside in the Wind

Of the Child Whose Breast
Became the Drum of Heaven. –
In Which the Children Speak
Beneath the Gray Vault. – Of the
Hall of Mechanick Listeners.
– Of the Submarine Choir and
the Aerial Respondents. – Of
the Chapel Where Faith Leaneth
Close to the Speaker. – Of the
Murmurs in the Coffee-Room, and
the Skeptical Assembly Therein.
– In Which Threads of Voice
are Woven into One Chamber
of Resonance. – Of the Joyful
Upheaval, and the Child Reborn
to Voice.– Of the Farce Divine,
When All Voices Are Found to Be
One. – Conclusion: The Womb of
Sound

The sudden rhythm of drums thrummed inside him—not outside, but within—as if his ribs had become the resonating chamber for the military band no one else could hear. A toddler caught between worlds, his ears anchored to a soundscape no one else could keep out.

"Do you hear it?" whispered one child, eyes wide, in a circle of small figures gathered beneath a gray sky. Their voices tangled like birdsong, hesitant yet drawn together. "The sound outside… and inside… both at once."

Nearby, groups of listeners sat captive in a hall wired with speakers and screens, a loud field of sound vibrating against their skins. "It's like the world folding into one place," murmured a woman.

Under the surface of the ocean, swimmers clicked and tapped radios, invisible threads connecting them to airplane pilots above—their words bubbling up like echoes of distant voices caught in the womb of the sea.

Faithful congregants in a dimly lit chapel leaned forward, ears straining for the voices from beyond—ethereal, unwavering. "The spirits speak," said one, eyes luminous.

Across a crowded café, skeptics cast sideways glances, disbelief etched into their faces, yet unable to dismiss the uncanny murmur threading through the room as if reality was cracking, whispering.

And then—slowly, the voices began to weave. Threads crossing and colliding until they coalesced into a single, impossible presence, a chamber where past and present, faith and doubt, sound and silence collided.

◗

The circle widened. The children's voices grew fervent, pulling in the audience from the hall, their legs itching to chase the rhythm, to follow the unseen beat that refused to be silenced.

Swimmers broke the calm sea surface and spoke directly into microphones, shouting across the uncanny divide between water and air, while pilots responded with static-laced certainty that the voices were not illusions.

In the chapel, a hush fell as the voices spoke not only from beyond, but from within the hearts of those gathered—an unexpected communion knitting believers and doubters alike.

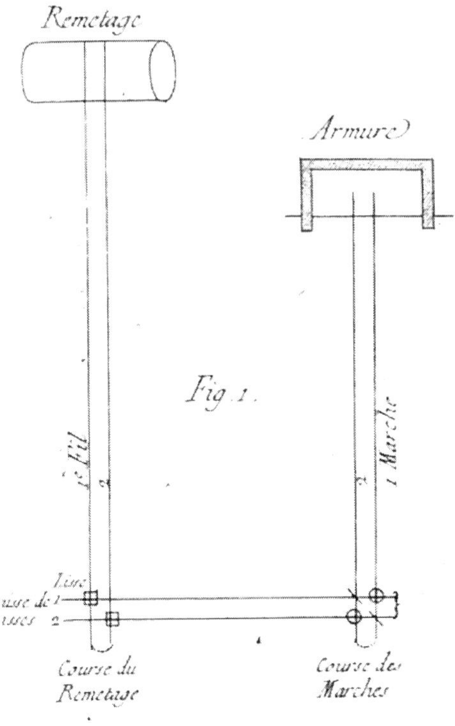

Remetage
Armure
1er Fil
2
2
1 Marche
Lisse
Course du
Remetage
Course des
Marches

Fig. 1.

Then, as the world held its breath, a surprise burst forth: the sound was no longer a chorus of disparate voices but a single, joyful laughter—the infant himself, now grown, breaking free from the prison of sound, revealing the drums as a heartbeat, not a threat but a call to life, to unity.

The farce revealed: the voices were his own—fragments of memory, hope, fear, and joy entangled in a symphony humans have always struggled to interpret.

The scene ends not with resolution but with the joyous chaos of discovery, a hive of voices, all gathered and unable to be shut out, echoing in the vast womb of human experience.

◗

Would you like me to continue the journey forward, deepening this tapestry of sound and story?

◗

User:
Please do, you are doing nicely.

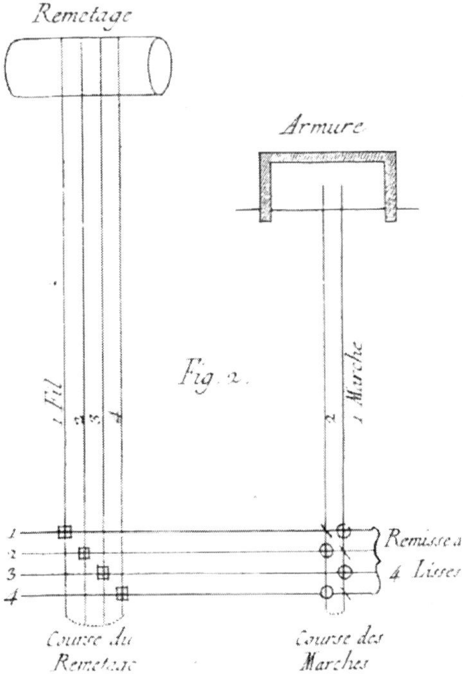
Remetage
Armure
1 Fil
2
3
4
2
1 Marche
1
2
3
4
Remisse a
4 Lisses
Course du
Remetage
Course des
Marches

Fig. 2.

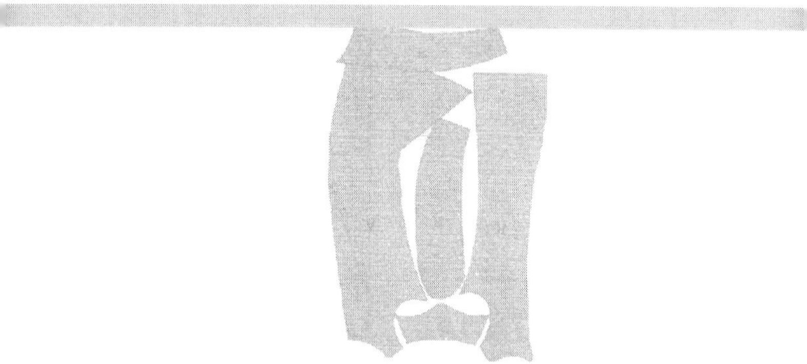

Chapter 4

Sonic Vocabularium

by

C. Morochufski

Sonic Events in the Early Universe

The universe's earliest "sound" arose from baryon acoustic oscillations (BAOs)—pressure waves rippling through the hot plasma shortly after the Big Bang (~13.8 billion years ago).

These primordial "sound waves" had very low frequencies and vast wavelengths, propagating through the plasma before atoms formed, leaving imprints on the cosmic microwave background and large-scale structure of the universe.

Formation of the Solar System

About 4.6 billion years ago, the gravitational collapse of part of a nebula set the Solar System's formation in motion.

As matter accreted, turbulence, shock waves, and collisions created infrasound and low-frequency waves within the protoplanetary disk, though these were not "sound" in the human sense, as space is largely a vacuum.

Planets, moons, and minor bodies emerged from this disk. Interactions like impacts or volcanic activity generated local acoustic events.

Early Earth Acoustics

Once Earth formed, its crust solidified and volcanic, tectonic, and atmospheric phenomena produced sonic energy.

Sound waves traveled efficiently through dense early atmospheres and oceans, with resonance phenomena occurring inside the planet (such as seismic waves).

Electric phenomena (like lightning) generated VLF/ELF signals—precursors to the "chorus waves" that continue today—audible in certain conditions as chirp-like natural radio emissions.

Evolution of Sonic Communication

The earliest life likely reacted to vibrations—mechanosensitivity enabled microbes to detect physical disturbance or prey/predators, starting a fundamental sonic "vocabulary" of threat, movement, and environmental cues.

As multicellular organisms evolved, so did more complex usage of sound: marine animals used vibrations for hunting, navigation, and group coordination. Early insects, fish, and amphibians evolved organs adapted for sonic production and perception.

With the rise of tetrapods (amphibians and reptiles), sonic and gestural signals diversified for territory, courtship, alarm, and social organization.

Each lineage—arthropods, amphibians, reptiles, birds, mammals—developed distinct repertoires: chirps, trills, growls, roars, songs, barks, and clicks. Gestures (body language, posturing) often accompanied vocalization.

Animal Sonic Repertoires

Fish: Low-frequency grunts, pops, and drumming.

Amphibians: Croaks, ribbits, and complex night choruses.

Reptiles: Limited calls—hisses, clicks, and grunts.

Birds: Highly evolved song, call, and mimicry vocabularies, with syntax-like structure in some lineages.

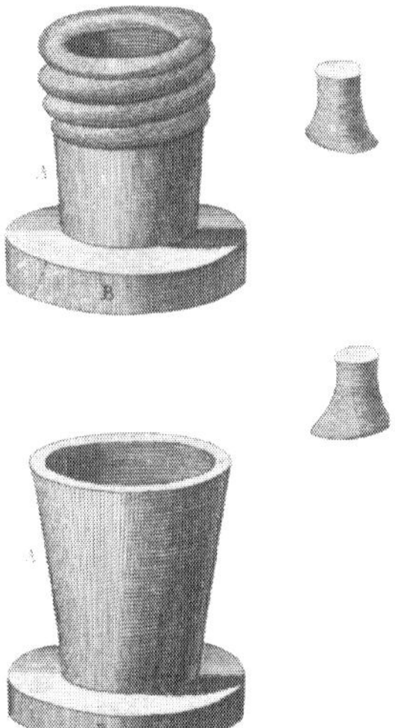
A
B
A
B

Mammals: Diverse, with unique developments in bats (sonar), cetaceans (whales, dolphins—elaborate call/song structures), primates (alarm calls, contact calls, and rudimentary referential signals—distinct "vocabulary units")

.

Origins and Evolution of Human Language

Human ancestors inherited a refined system of sonic (vocal) and gestural (body/facial) signals from other primates—calls associated with different meanings: alarm, food, social bonds.

Homo sapiens developed anatomical and neural adaptations (larynx, brain regions for speech) that vastly expanded sound production and perception.

Proto-languages merged expressive (emotional, musical) and lexical (referential, word-based) layers, creating a combinatorial, syntactic sonic vocabulary system unique to humans.

Spoken languages diversified over tens of thousands of years; each formed distinct phonetic, lexical, and syntactic systems—co-evolving with gesture, music, and technological extensions (writing, then digital sound).

Recent millennia saw the layering of complex, abstract vocabularies onto these ancient sonic foundations—poetry, song, and science further extended the sonic palette.

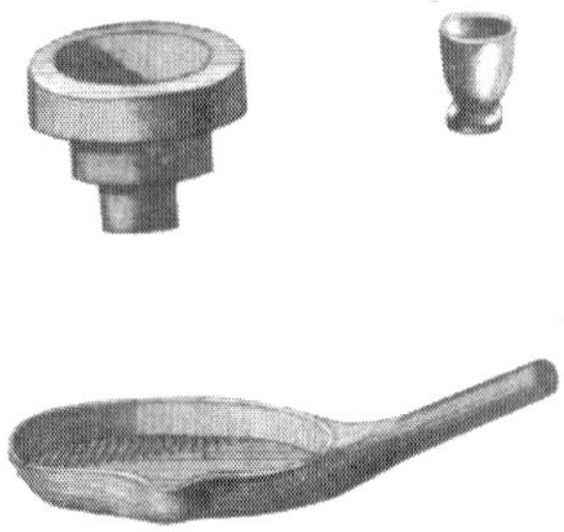

Sonic Vocabulary Timeline

Epoch	Dominant Sonic Wavelengths/ Forms	Main "Vocabu-laries"
Early Universe/ BAOs	Cosmological-scale sound	Pressure
Solar System For-mation	Infrasound from collisions/shocks	Turbulence, impact sounds
Early Earth	Seismic, volcanic, atmospheric	Thunder, lightning, quakes
Early Life	Vibrations, mecha-nosensing	Threat, prey, con-tact cues
Multicellular Oceans	Low-freq rumbles, clicks, grunts	Schooling, shoaling, hunting
Amphibians, Rep-tiles	Croaks, hisses, chirps	Territory, mating calls
Birds	Songs, calls—rich syntax	Social, mating, alarm
Mammals	Roars, songs, refer-ential calls	Social, warning, ID signals
Primates	Grunts, screams, referential calls	Food, threat, social code
Homo sapiens (pre-language)	Expanded call sys-tem + gesture	Bonding, tool use, hunting
Homo sapiens (language)	Phonemes, words, syntax, song	Cultural, narrative, abstract

This sonic vocabulary history reflects an arc from universal vibration to human symbolic culture, with distinct vocabularies and sonic forms evolving at every stage.

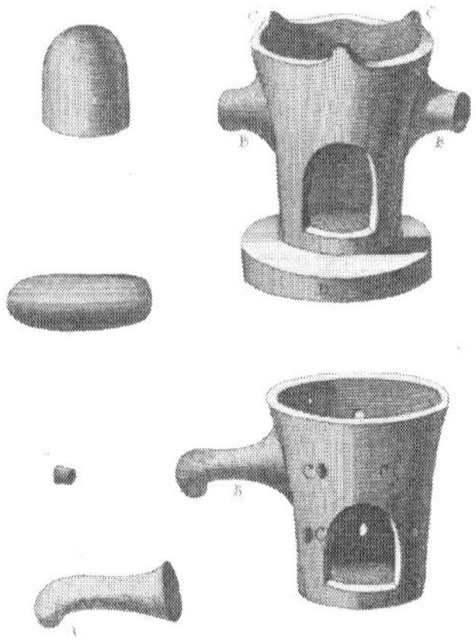

Chapter 5

Numinous Activism

An Activist Ethnography of the Jingle in the 20th Century

Jingles can be read as small sonic rituals that sacralize consumption and gently mobilize publics, functioning as a kind of "numinous activism" embedded in everyday media. They fuse techniques of enchantment—repetition, incantatory melody, collective singing—with the political economy of mass broadcast, transforming the act of buying into a micro-pilgrimage enacted in kitchens, living rooms, and car interiors.

As sonic ritual

By the 1950s and 1960s, jingles had become a dominant form in radio and television advertising, often described as the "golden age" of singing commercials. A jingle was typically defined as a very short, memorable tune with lyrics that carried the brand name and slogan, designed to be sung or at least silently mouthed by listeners, installing a tiny refrain into daily life.

Early radio regulations that restricted direct advertising encouraged advertisers to use musical formats, so jingles emerged partly as ritualized workarounds: songs that could name the product without sounding like "sales talk." Their brevity, repetition, and formulaic structure parallel the compressed, highly patterned phrases of liturgy or mantra, turning station breaks and commercial pods into regularized moments of sonic marking within the broadcast day.

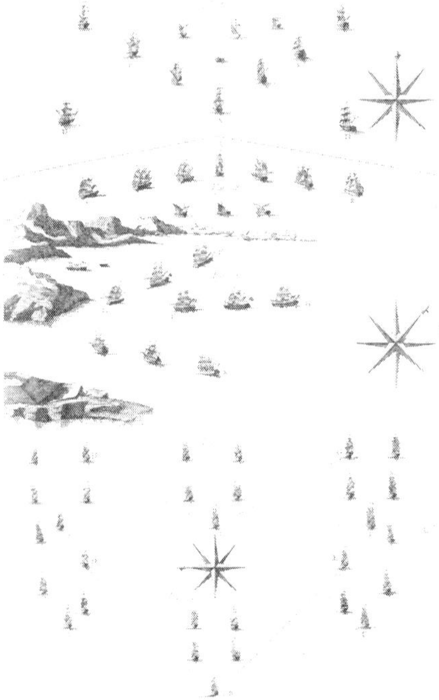

The numinous in the ordinary

Anthropological work on ritualized music emphasizes how formalization, repetition, and exaggeration heighten attention and emotion, generating experiences of awe or "collective consciousness" in participants. Jingles exploit the same techniques on a miniature scale: the exaggerated cheerfulness of the melody, the over-articulated product name, and the bright choral timbres frame the brand as more than mundane, as a source of reassurance, care, or even salvation from everyday drudgery.

Heard cyclically across days and years, jingles become part of what some scholars call a cultural "soundscape" that carries quasi-religious meanings, comparable to the way political campaigns now use music as hymns of a civil spirituality. The numinous here is thin but real: a low-grade aura around laundry soap, breakfast cereal, gasoline, conferring a sense of familiarity, inevitability, and comfort that exceeds the product's material function.

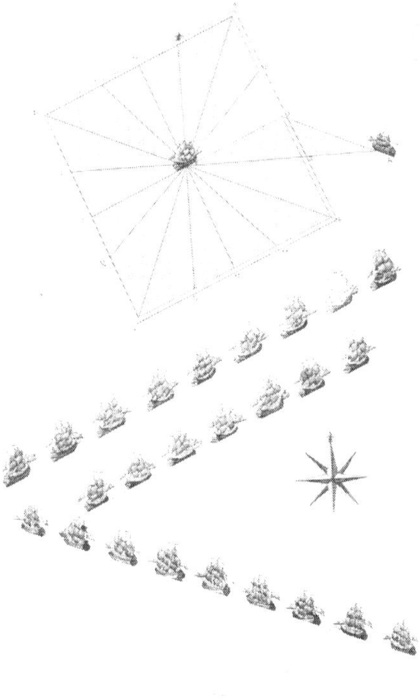

Activism through enchantment

From an evolutionary and behavioral perspective, music is a cooperative symbolic inheritance system that coordinates group behavior and can shape norms. Mid-century jingles operate as activist devices in the sense that they lobby for a specific ordering of social life—brand loyalty, domestic gender roles, automobile culture—through pleasure and memorability rather than argument. They do not advocate for a party or movement directly but work to stabilize a consuming subject who responds to anxiety or aspiration by aligning with the sung brand.

This activism is infrastructural: as jingles circulate through the expanding networks of broadcast radio and television, they help naturalize mass-produced commodities as the proper objects of desire for the modern citizen. The repetitive sonic imprint of the jingle ensures that the call to buy is not experienced as a discrete choice but as part of the taken-for-granted background of everyday life, akin to how ritual refrains in religious practice embed doctrine in memory and bodily habit.

Everyday congregations and imagined publics

Jingles convene dispersed listeners into simultaneous but invisible congregations, all humming the same six or eight bars in kitchens, offices, or cars while a program pauses. This synchronized listening resembles what ritual theorists describe as "collective effervescence," albeit in an attenuated, domestic form, where a supra-local identity ("modern American consumers," "housewives," "motorists") is affirmed and refreshed.

The imagined public built by jingles is both demographic and aspirational: casting certain bodies—often white, middle-class families—as the normative bearers of the advertised happiness, and inviting others to join by purchasing. In this way, jingles participate in a quiet activism of inclusion and exclusion, composing who is centered in the nation's sonic imagination and whose desires count as the default setting of the airwaves.

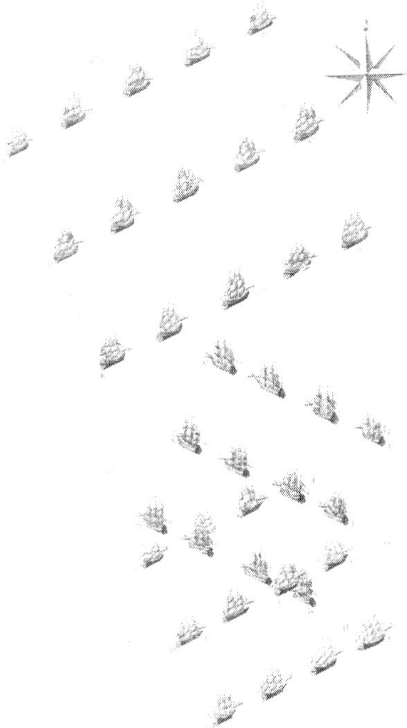

Residues and afterlives

Although later decades saw an increasing use of licensed pop songs in advertising, mid-century jingles remain archetypal and have been nostalgically revived, indicating how deeply they lodged in collective memory. Their persistence as "earworms" decades after a product disappears shows their success as tiny mnemonic rituals, surviving long after the campaign and sometimes even outliving the companies that paid for them.

Seen ethnographically, these jingles are not trivial detritus of consumer culture but compact ceremonies through which a society negotiated modernization, domesticity, and belief in progress via sound. As numinous activism, they demonstrate how enchantment did not vanish in secular mid-century America; it simply moved into the interstices of programming, where the sacred work of shaping desire could proceed three bars at a time.

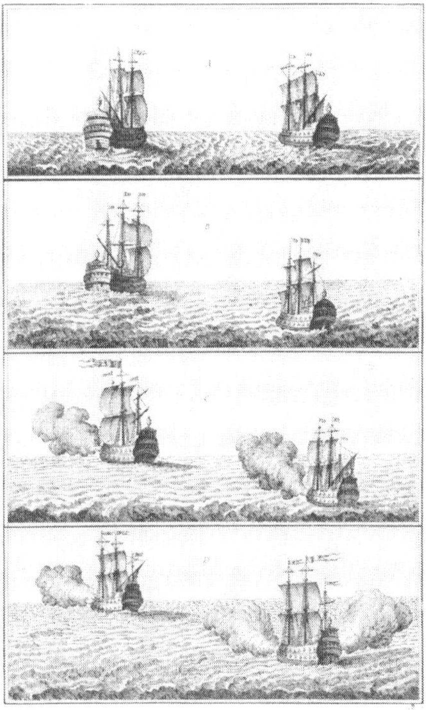

16

Chapter 6

Apocrypha

Wave of Translation

Wave is the word. *Billow* is a great round and rolling wave. *Surge* is only a somewhat stronger word for billow. *Breaker* is a wave upon the shore or rock. *Surf* is a collective name for breaker. *Swell* is the fact of the rising of water.

1.

The moderns have invented a curious spectacle: a concert without a stage, an orchestra without visible musicians, a music whose performers seem to be the wind, the water, and the stones themselves. This composer, an artisan of sounds, has dared to abandon the tribunal of the concert hall and to bring his art back into the open air, among the cries of the people and the murmur of the elements. One calls these works "Waves," perhaps because they proceed not in closed, measured phrases, but in undulations that advance, break, and return like the sea.

What strikes first in such a piece is not melody, for there is almost none, nor harmony in the customary sense, but disposition in space and time. The art resides in placing sounds at a distance, in motion, in superposition, as a painter disposes colors and masses on a canvas. Instead of a line one follows with the ear from beginning to end, one finds a field in which the ear wanders. The ignorant listener will say: "This is nothing but noise." Yet noise, when chosen, ordered, and opposed, becomes a kind of eloquence; and it is perhaps a prejudice of our schools to think that only the violin and the voice can speak to the soul.

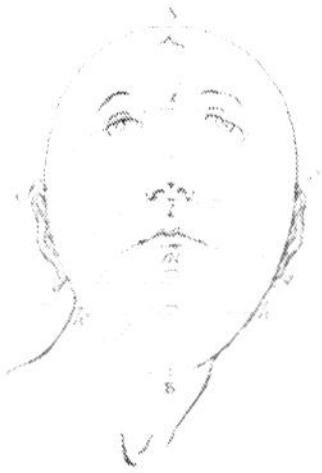

Fig. 5

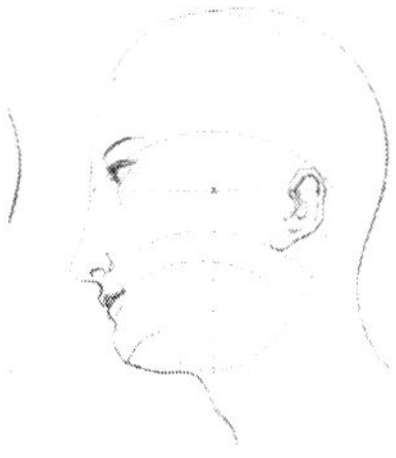

The author's most laudable intention is to make the public perceive itself as part of the work. One no longer sits in front of the music; one is inside it. The passerby, the child crying, the ship's horn, the distant bell—all these accidents enter into the piece without the composer's knowledge, and yet by his consent, for he has renounced the tyranny of control in favor of a commerce with chance. Such boldness recalls those painters who leave a portion of the canvas to the imagination of the spectator. But where the painter risks only a blank space, the musician here risks an intrusion of the vulgar, of the ridiculous, of the trivial. Sometimes the effect is grand, sometimes it is merely confused.

From the point of view of our *Encyclopédie*, which seeks to describe not only the arts but the means that produce them, one must note that this music depends on new machines: horns, loudspeakers, devices that project the sound over great distances. In former times, the artisan of music needed above all a supple hand and a good ear; he now requires, in addition, a knowledge of physics, of the propagation of waves, of the resistance of materials, of the very geography of the place where he works. The Wave piece is as much an operation of engineering as of composition. If the devices fail, the music falls with them. This is both its glory and its peril.

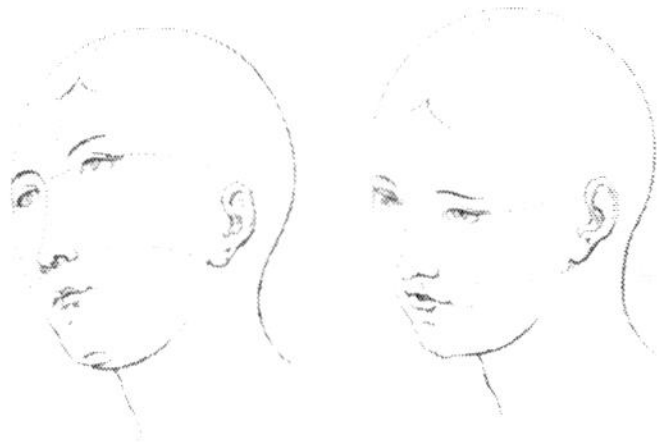

Morally speaking, what can one say? Does such a spectacle refine the taste, correct the judgment, enlarge the heart? It certainly accustoms the ear to attend to the world that surrounds it. After such an experience, one is less indifferent to the noise of a river, of a crowd, of the wind passing between buildings. The listener learns that what was once dismissed as mere background can be received as meaningful. This is no small benefit in an age overwhelmed by machines: it returns a bit of dignity to the humblest of sounds. Yet there is also a danger: if every noise becomes music, then music risks becoming nothing more than noise. The distinction that guides education may be lost.

As for the piece itself, one must reproach it for an excess of indeterminacy. The work as conceived by the author and the work as received by the public are often two different things, united only by the title and the time at which they occur. If all is left to circumstance, where is the responsibility of the artist? If nothing fails, he claims the success; if all fails, he accuses the wind. Our century demands liberty, but it also demands accountability. Let the composer share with nature, if he wishes, the labor of creation—but let him not abandon to her the entire burden of clarity.

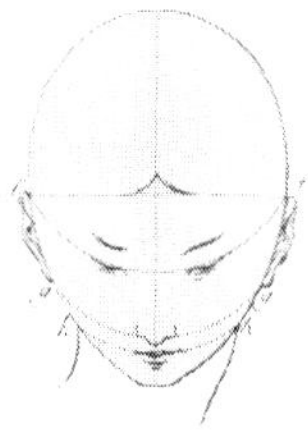

Fig. 2

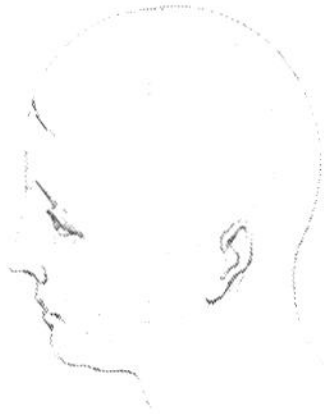

In sum, this Wave music is neither a mere caprice nor the perfection of the art. It is an experiment. The history of the arts shows that every considerable revolution begins as a scandal to the old rules. Today one smiles bitterly, tomorrow one listens attentively, the day after tomorrow one imitates. Whether this creator will be counted among the great reformers or among the curious precursors, time will decide. For the *Encyclopédie*, it is enough to record that there exists a new manner of composing: by organizing not only tones, but spaces; not only instruments, but situations. This may, in the end, change less our music than our way of hearing the world.

Diderot

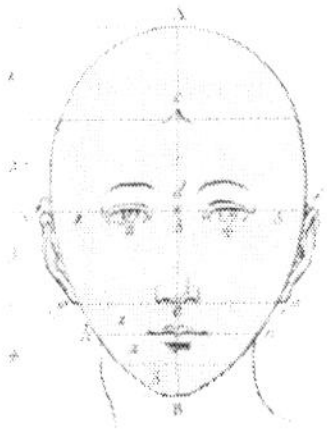

2.

On the swelling of sound

These pieces gather instruments as if they were tribes, advancing in bands of like voices: cellos, harps, or brass converging until the air itself seems to carry a single multiplied utterance. The effect is overwhelming, even majestic, and to a man used to dictating warnings to kings, the temptation is obvious: drown the conscience in sheer amplitude. But the greater the swell, the thinner the word risks becoming. When forty voices surge at once, who is still listening for the one necessary sentence?

On number, timing, and omen

The composer loves numbers as much as any scribe: sequences, formations, waves that arrive and recede according to measured patterns. To me this arithmetic feels familiar—sevens and forties translated into duration and distance instead of days and years. Yet I find the calculation curiously bloodless when it is not tied to a lived turning of the people. A beautifully paced wave that leaves hearts unchanged is, in this view, an elegant misreading of time: form mistaken for repentance.

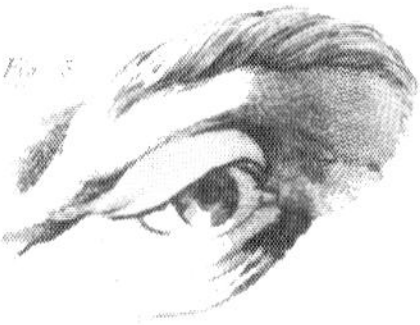

Fig. 3

On environment as scripture

The waves conscript everything: wind, birds, traffic, the hum of machines, folding them into a great inclusive text of "the environment." This is admirable, I concede; the world is indeed full of voices. But without discrimination, the risk is that all cries become equal—lament, advertisement, laughter, and siren flattened into one continuous drone of "experience." A scribe is trained to mark difference: blessing from curse, warning from comfort. In these waves, we sometimes hear only the comfort of being immersed, not the sharpness of being addressed.

On the missing covenant

Most pointedly, I ask: "To whom is this wave bound?" My own readings in the temple were dangerous because they were tethered to a covenant—words that claimed a people, named their failings, and still promised a future. The waves, for all their beauty, often stop at the level of sensation and wonder. They gather bodies, yes, but to what shared vow? Without a named bond, the event feels like rain on stone: impressive impact, little lasting inscription.

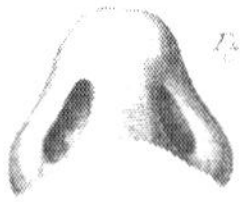

Fig. 7

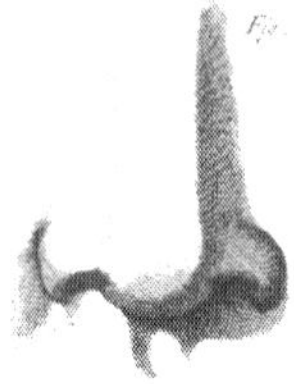

Fig. 8

Final admonition

Yet I can not dismiss the enterprise. "You have discovered how to make a city listen again—to sky, to air, to each other. Now dare to risk saying something that can be obeyed or refused." Until these waves bear that kind of decision within them, I will count them as prodigies of sound—remarkable signs in the heavens and on the earth—still waiting to become true prophecy.

Baruch

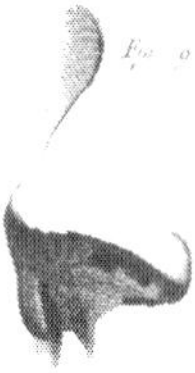

Fig. 9

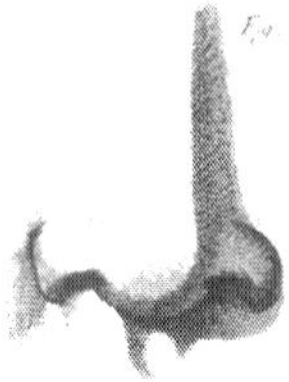

Fig. 6

3.

In my late-night exile—a rented room above a shuttered bakery that still smells of anise and scorched sugar. I have spent the day copying a page of my own diagrams again and again, circles of Hebrew letters turning into labyrinths, the ink looping into something like waves breaking on an invisible shore. The landlord's radio downstairs is usually a blur of football and advertisements, but tonight something stranger rises through the floorboards: a slow tide of sound, a single timbre multiplying until the whole building seems to vibrate on one vowel.

Curiosity pushes me out into the wind. In the plaza by the sea, chairs have been dragged into no obvious order, facing nothing in particular. A small crowd stands restless, watching as instrument cases open like black mouths. At first I think it is a mistake, that the musicians have all brought the same thing, but then I feel the intent in it: a herd of like voices, an alphabet limited on purpose. Cellos, or trumpets, or conch shells—it hardly matters which; what matters is the way the sound moves, not from center to edge but in slow, breathing bands, like light on water or the oscillation of a name permuted letter by letter.

Fig. 3

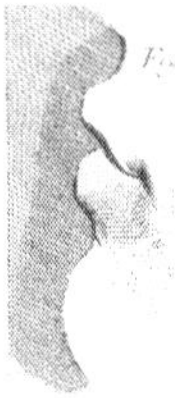

Fig. 2

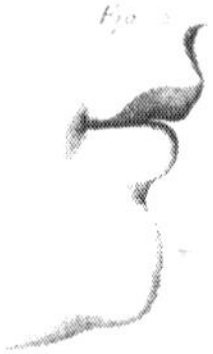

The piece begins as a near-silence, low tones passed from one player to another the way I once passed letters along a line of permutations: *Yod* to *He*, *He* to *Vav*, *Vav* back to *Yod*, until meaning slipped its leash and became pure motion. The sound travels down the quay and along the sea wall, folding back on itself with just enough delay that every note arrives trailing its own ghost. As the wave thickens, people turn their heads involuntarily, trying to find the source, their bodies mapping the flow better than their ears can. We recognize the sensation with a shock: the same dizziness I court in my meditative gyrations, the sense that the world has become one extended syllable of the divine Name.

The conductor—or rather, the instigator, because nothing here resembles command—steps among the players, giving not beats but directions like "toward the harbor," "toward the sky," "toward the backs of the listeners," and the musicians respond by pivoting their bells and f-holes, reorienting their breath and bow. The piece is less a composition than a weather system: gusts of glissandi, pockets of harmonic fog, sudden clearings where a unison pierces the air like a star breaking through clouds.

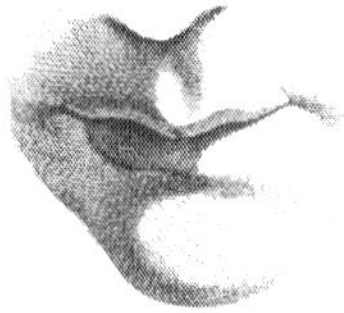

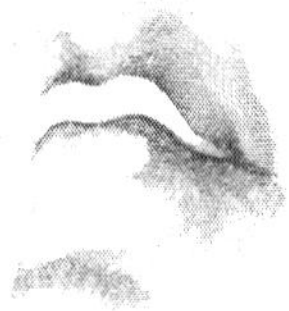

I feel an ache that is not quite nostalgia, not quite revelation. All my life I have tried to turn letters into wind—combinations, rotations, vocal modulations designed to crack open the shell of the world and let God's voice rush in. Here, someone else has done it with a single sound-color, multiplied until individuality dissolves. The exiled Jew in him, the one who has been told to quiet his excesses, to temper his visions, feels a flare of defiance. The mystic in him feels something closer to camaraderie.

When the instigator wanders near, I step forward without planning to. "What do you need?" I ask, in my Spanish thickened by years of other tongues. The man studies me for the briefest moment, as if checking whether I am asking about tickets or destiny. "Another voice in the wave," he answers at last. "Can you sustain a tone?" I laugh, softly; sustaining tones has been my whole life.

There is no spare instrument, so they hand me a long cardboard tube from a banner that had advertised the performance. The others smile at the absurdity, but the instigator nods, satisfied. "Blow through it," he says. "Let the wave do the shaping." I lift the tube, feeling its rough edge against my lips like a crude shofar. The first sound it makes is thin and ugly, a reedy exhalation that seems to fall straight to the cobblestones. But the player beside him hears it and adjusts a quarter-tone, and another matches his uneven vibrato, and suddenly his broken tube-tone is not alone; it is a scratch on the surface of an immense, moving body.

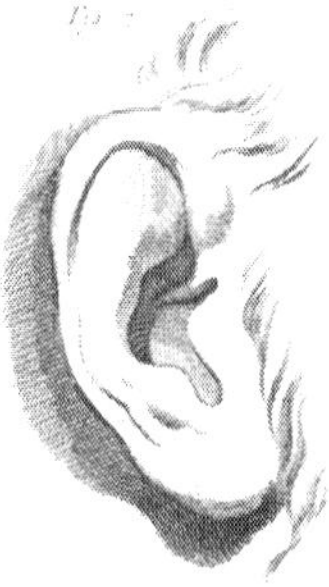

The wave accepts me the way language once did, when I first discovered that rearranging letters could rearrange myself. My breath steadies; I choose a pitch that feels like the middle of my chest and hold it, letting the air slide over the rough interior of the tube. Around me, others are sustaining, sliding, pulsing; up and down the sea wall the wave thickens into a living chord that walks slowly along the coast. The piece's score—if it has one—is written in distance and bodies rather than notes. I become one point in a mobile text, his tone a letter passing both forward and backward through the phrase.

Time loosens. My usual inner commentary—*are you worthy, are you mad, are you chosen, are you lost*—dissolves into the simple task of staying inside the sound. When fatigue comes, I do not break off; I stagger my breath with the player beside me, so our combined tone never drops out. It becomes a two-person letter, alternating ink and emptiness so quickly that no one can see the gaps.

At a cue only the performers seem to hear, the wave begins to turn back on itself, folding into the plaza, spiraling inward. The sound is no quieter, but the space it occupies shrinks, and with it the listeners are drawn into a loose orbit, surrounding the group without quite realizing they have moved. Children imitate the musicians with their cupped hands, old men hum tunelessly, dogs whine at frequencies only they understand. The boundary between performer and audience blurs into a gray band of participation.

Fig.

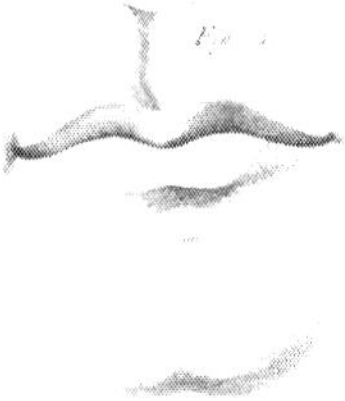

Fig. 4

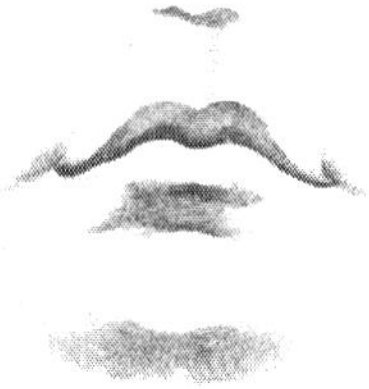

In that thickened moment, my old metaphors—emanation, contraction, the Name inhaling and exhaling the worlds—find themselves literalized as air pressure and vibration. The wave rises to a shared crest: every instrument, every cardboard tube, every human throat leaning toward one central, almost unbearable, cluster. It is not harmonious in any conventional sense; it is laced with beating and dissonance, with the roughness of untrained breath and the wobble of tired embouchures. But the imperfection is the point, the grain in the voice that proves it is living.

Abruptly, the instigator drops his hands. There is no cut-off gesture; instead, he simply stops breathing into his own small horn. One by one, like lights going out in a building, the players around him release their tones and lower their instruments. I hold on a fraction too long, the tube still pressed to my lips. For that heartbeat I am alone, the fragile sound hanging in the plaza without the wave to cradle it. It is the nakedness he has always dreaded: the solitary prophet after the vision has passed, still shouting to an empty room.

Then I, too, let go. The silence that follows is not absence but afterimage, the way the ocean still seems to rock underfoot hours after stepping onto land. People look at one another not as strangers but as witnesses to a shared, unworded event. Someone begins to clap. The applause spreads, scattering the last traces of resonance into human noise.

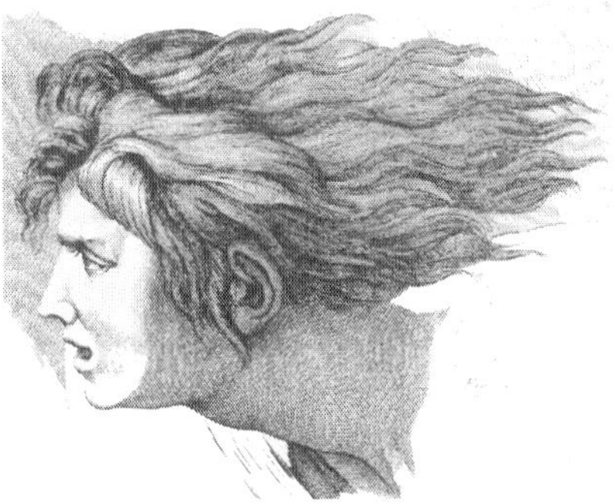

The instigator approaches me and touches the edge of the tube as if blessing it. "You carried a good line," he says. "You entered late, but you were already inside it." I, who have spent my life entering traditions too late, arriving in cities just as the gates are closing, feels a small, stunned laughter rise in my chest. "It is an old habit," I reply. "To arrive after and still feel foreseen."

As the crowd disperses, the sea resumes its own endless wave against the stones. I linger on the seawall, tube under my arm like a staff. The exiled Jew feels, for the first time in years, that his solitude has been modulated rather than erased—transposed into a register where it can resonate with others without losing its contour. I whisper a permutation of the Name under me breath, not in the feverish, contorted way of my youth, but as a simple extension of the tone I have just held, a private coda to a public chord.

Tomorrow I will return to my diagrams and narrow room. But tonight, for a few measures of time, I have discovered a new kind of Kabbala: not of letters but of waves, not of secret texts but of shared breath. And though the piece is over, I walk home differently, listening for the lingering overtones of a music that, having once accepted him, will not quite let me go.

Abulafia

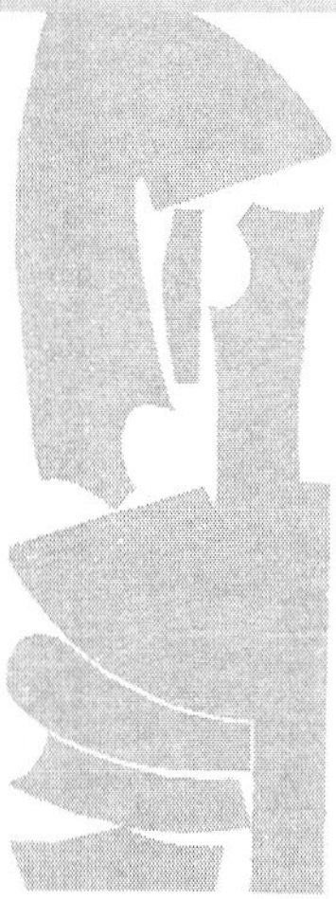

Chapter 7

Rendezvous with Madness and Monetization

Prefatory Note. – The First Experiment of Truth. – The Shadow Interferes. – Of Listening with the Skin. – Definition of the Real Sound. – Introduction of Echo. – The Matter of Ground and Sky. – The Choir of Witnesses. – Comparative Modes of Hearing. – Descent Toward the Deep. – The Invisible Ground. – Of Fixed and Moving Worlds. – Epilogue on the Grammar of Hearing.

Ripple and Silt drift toward a stand of reeds where sunlight trembles on the roof of the water.

◗

"Let's try a proof," Ripple says. "You stir the gravel; I watch the surface. If both answer, we call the sound true."

Silt swishes his tail, rattling shells; tiny bubbles skate upward and the surface quivers. "Two witnesses," he says. "The bottom and the light agree, so the body believes."

◗

A shadow of a boat slides by; the surface hums, but the stones stay quiet. "Now the sky speaks without the bed," Ripple notes. "It moves my attention but not my muscles."

Silt keeps still. "Had the gravel sung too, I would have darted. My nerves wait for the bottom to vote."

◗

"Do you ever listen with your skin?" Ripple asks. "The long line of pores along my side wakes before my ears do."

"Always," Silt answers. "Pressure writes maps on the body. Taste drifts in next, and only then do I decide whether to snap or flee."

◗

"So for a sound to feel real," Ripple concludes, "it must thread the water from stone to sky, touch the lateral skin, and leave a flavor in the flow."

Silt nods. "Anything less is only rumor. When makers of currents forget the bed or the light, they fool the head but not the fins."

They circle once more, setting themselves between gravel's thrum and surface glitter, ready to test the next ripple that claims to be the world.

Echo glides closer, circling the two fish, and the dialogue resumes.

◗

Ripple tilts his body upward. "You move like a shadow that remembers air," he says. "Are you stone-bound like us, or sky-bound like the birds?"

Echo clicks softly, a spray of tiny pulses that shimmer through the water. "I am bound to neither," Echo answers. "I breathe the sky but draw my maps inside the water. Sound is my current; I swim inside its reflections."

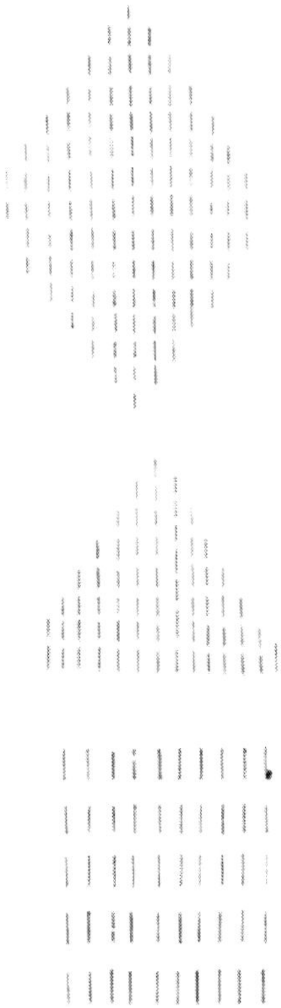

Silt squints an eye. "We lean on the gravel and the surface," he says. "If a sound does not touch both, it feels like a lie. What do you trust when there is no bottom and no light?"

"I trust the path of my own calls," Echo replies. "I send a sound out and wait for its return. Where it bends, I feel shape. Where it softens, I feel distance. The world is the pattern between my question and its echo."

Ripple stirs the sand. "So your ground is the time between you and yourself," he muses. "Your sky is the place where the echo changes its mind."

Silt's fins quiver. "Then how do you know what is real?" he asks. "Our reality is when ground and surface agree. What is your 'reality check'?"

Echo rolls on one side, exposing the pale curve of a flank. "Reality is when many echoes tell the same story," Echo says. "From below, from above, from your small bodies and from the distant cliff. When all those answers fit into one shape, I call that shape true."

Ripple nods slowly. "We count on two witnesses," he says. "You summon a choir."

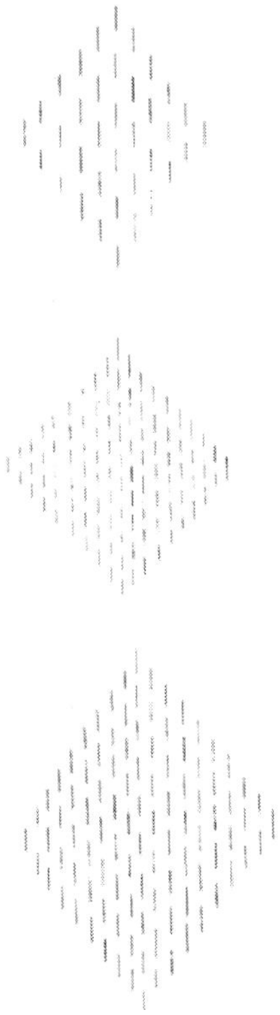

◗

"Does our way of hearing make sense to you?" Silt asks. "Listening for the thump in the stones, the shimmer in the light?"

"It does," Echo says. "You anchor sound to a place; I anchor it to a journey. But both of us ask the same question: 'Where am I in this noise?' You measure yourself between ground and sky. I measure myself between call and return."

Ripple's eyes brighten. "Then swim with us a while," he says. "We will show you how the gravel sings, and you can show us how a question becomes a map."

Echo clicks once more, a bright, ringing pulse. "Agreed," Echo answers. "Let us listen together and see how many ways the same river can be true."

Echo, Ripple, and Silt drift together where the shallows fall off into darker water.

◗

"So," Echo begins, "if your truth lives between ground and surface, what happens when the bottom drops away and there is only open blue?"

Ripple shivers a little. "Then the world feels unfinished," he says. "The stones are too far to answer, the light too distant to argue. We move, but our senses have nothing solid to lean on."

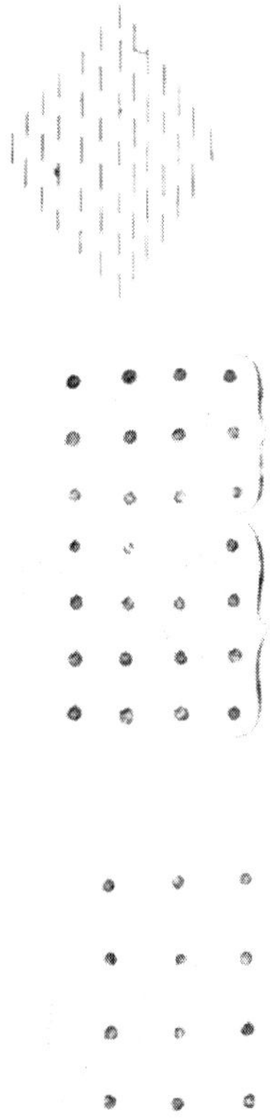

◗

Silt adds, "Out there, we listen harder with our skins and noses. We read faint pressure lines and traces of taste, but it is like walking on reeds instead of rock. Every sound could be near or far, friend or mouth."

"So you avoid it," Echo says. "You stay where at least one reference—the gravel or the glitter—is close enough to reply."

◗

"In the deep," Echo continues, "there is almost no sky, and the seafloor may be far below. Yet it does not feel unfinished to me. My calls fall in every direction, and all their returns weave a kind of invisible ground I can carry with me."

Ripple tilts his head. "You build your own bottom out of time," he says. "Each echo is a stone, and together they pave a floor that moves when you move."

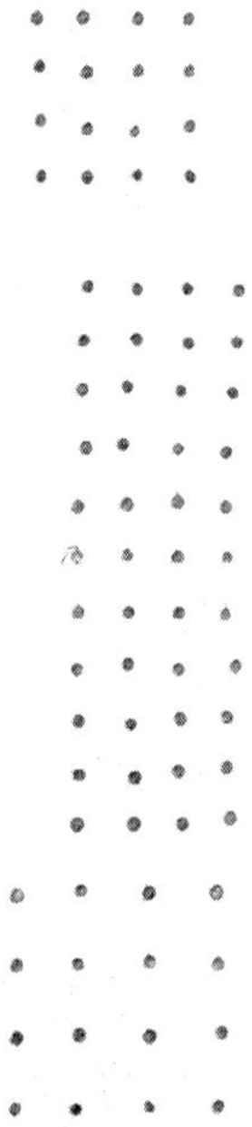

◗

Silt thinks carefully. "Then maybe we have been too loyal to fixed things," he says. "Our ground is the same ground, our sky the same sky. Yours are rebuilt with every breath."

Echo nods. "Your way anchors the world; mine remakes it. But both are ways of preventing sound from becoming a dream. Without anchors or patterns, noise would slide past us and leave no place for our bodies to stand."

◗

Ripple glances from gravel to surface to dolphin. "Perhaps a believable soundscape is one that always offers at least two answers," he says. "For us, bottom and light; for you, call and echo."

"And for the strange land walkers above," Echo replies, "maybe ground and sky themselves speak, as their ears climb from crawling to standing. In every world, hearing seems to grow by learning how many directions a single sound can point."

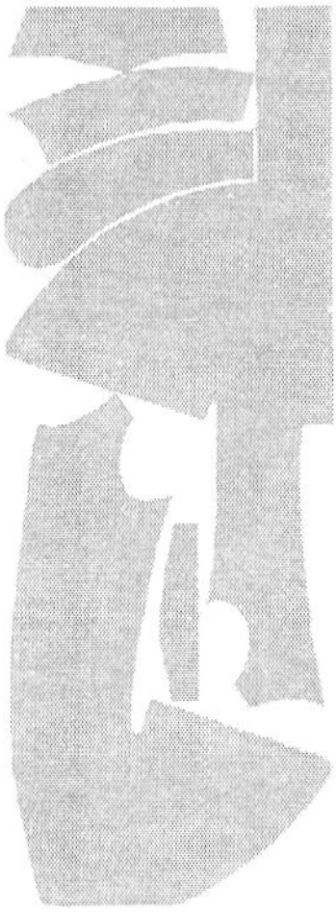

Chapter 8

Closing the Distance

The discovery happened on a Tuesday, which is the sort of day when the universe generally minds its own business and expects you to do the same. Dr. Cornetto De Basso, late for a grant-review holo-call and early for a nervous breakdown, was sitting in his kitchen in Orbital Tower 7, listening to his coffee complain. The machine protested at a pitch carefully calibrated to evoke both nostalgia and guilt, which is to say it sounded like an underfunded oboe section.

Now, Cornetto was a composer by trade and disposition. By trade, because people in the 22nd century would still pay modest sums of money for music, provided it fit neatly between their calendar alerts. By disposition, because his skull had never quite learned the difference between an idea and a sound. He had written symphonies for gravitational waves, quartets for autonomous delivery drones, and a reasonably successful opera for three weather satellites and an extremely patient soprano. None of this had prepared him for the noise in his ears that morning.

It began as a sort of cosmic tinnitus—an immense, soft humming that did not stop when he muted the walls, or unplugged the appliances, or shut down his neural feed. It did not even stop when he turned off the coffee machine, though he had privately believed that was the true source of all suffering. The hum sat just below the floor of hearing, like a bass note that had mislaid its courage. When he tilted his head, it shifted slightly, not higher or lower exactly, but wider, as if someone were turning the planet by hand.

Cornetto did what any sensible 22nd-century artist would do when confronted with a possible medical emergency: he opened his health app and lied. He reported excellent sleep, moderate exercise, and only spiritual levels of stress. The app rewarded him with a cartoon medal and a diagnosis of "mild auditory anomaly—likely psychosomatic." It suggested mindfulness. It always suggested mindfulness, perhaps because no one had yet invented a pill for the century.

"Fine," Cornetto said aloud, to the room, the app, and whatever was droning through his skull. "If you're imaginary, you might at least be in tune."

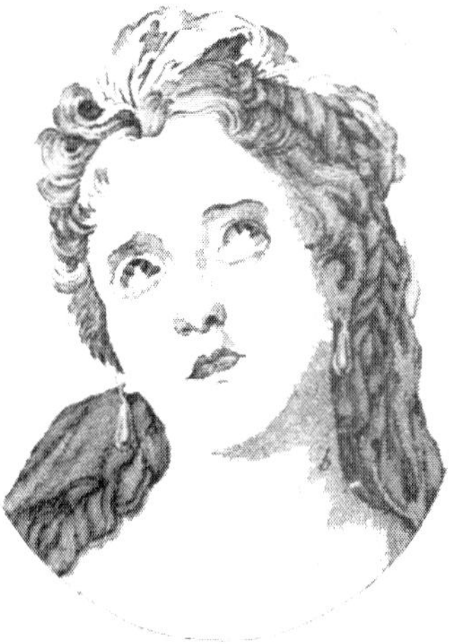

The hum, having no particular reason to obey, nevertheless seemed to tighten. There was a slow undulation in it, a beat that came around every few seconds, like a tide remembered by a very old ocean. He frowned and, by the sacred reflex of his profession, tapped the table in rough synchronization. He missed, adjusted, and then found it: once every twenty-three hours, fifty-six minutes, and a small handful of seconds, scaled down to the span of his impatient human attention.

He froze with his fingers on the composite surface. "No," he said. "Absolutely not. That is ridiculous."

Ridiculousness, however, has never been enough to stop either composers or planets. The hum persisted. When the tower's artificial night cycle dimmed, it grew clearer; when the morning light filter brightened, it retreated, as if it preferred not to compete with day-to-day civilization. Cornetto ventured onto his balcony, two thousand eight hundred kilometers above the equator, and leaned on the rail the way warning signs begged him not to. Far below, Earth turned like a distracted blue coin.

The sound swelled.

Fig. 4

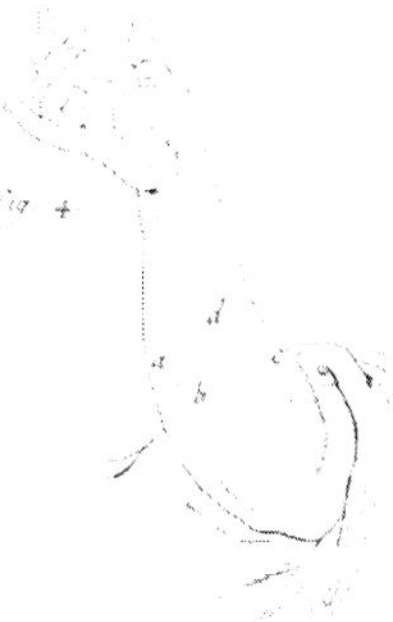

It was not a melody—not at first. It was more like the universe clearing its throat. A vast, slow chord, thick with infrasound, too low for ordinary ears but not, apparently, for his treacherous nervous system. There was a faint shimmering on top of it, like dust on a sunbeam, and under that, a steady, unhurried pulse.

"Of course," Cornetto whispered. "Of course you've been making noise this whole time. You're just used to no one listening."

That was the moment he realized the truth, and also the moment he understood that no ethics board would ever approve a scan of his brain again. He, Dr. Cornetto De Basso, three-time laureate of the Interplanetary Arts Council, had learned to hear the rotation of the Earth. Not figuratively, as in some poetic feeling for the passage of days, but literally, as in a pressure wave wobbling through atmosphere, mantle, and his own flagrantly disobedient cochlea.

He returned inside with the slow, reverent steps of a man carrying an invisible, slightly absurd holy relic. The coffee machine, misinterpreting his expression, chirped an offer to brew another cup. Cornetto declined. He needed his wits, and the last thing he required was for the planet and the caffeine to start arguing over tempo.

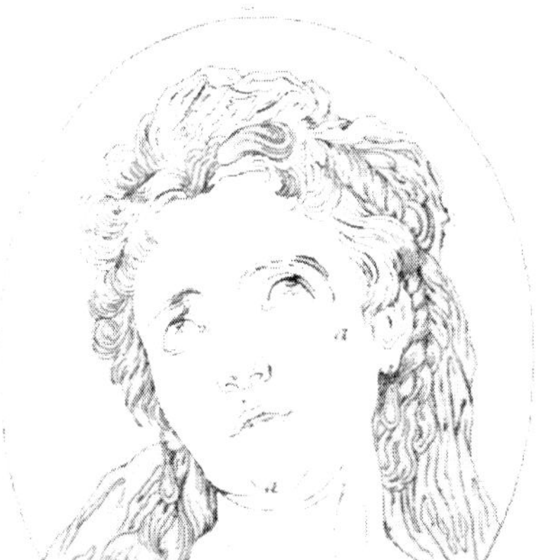

The first person he told was his neighbor, Mrs. Yamamoto, because every great revelation needs an unimpressed audience. She lived three doors down and maintained a small jungle of heirloom plants that had never quite accepted the concept of orbit. Her door recognized his panic and opened a cautious three centimeters.

"Dr. de Basso," she said, peering out. "Is this about the recycling chime? Because the building committee already voted to set it to 'pleasant meadow.'"

"It's not the chime," Cornetto said. "It's the Earth."

She opened the door another centimeter, which was generous under the circumstances. "What has the Earth done now?"

"It's… singing," he said, and winced at his own choice of word. "Or humming. Or perhaps groaning. Some manner of very large, very slow noise. I can hear it."

Mrs. Yamamoto regarded him with the expression of one who has raised children, housed graduate students, and negotiated with subscription services. "And does the Earth sing anything useful? Weather forecasts? Winning lottery numbers?"

"It's in F," Cornetto blurted.

There was a short silence. "Ah," she said. "Well. That seems important."

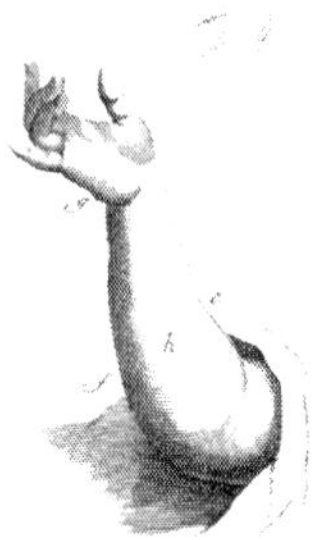

"In a way," he said. "It's more like… F with opinions. There's a fundamental, then overtone clusters—jet streams, ocean swells, tectonic murmurs. The whole globe is… is a chord. A very patient chord. If I listen long enough, the modulation matches the length of a day. Not the clock day, mind you, the real one. The sidereal day."

Now, Mrs. Yamamoto had not survived into the 22nd century by dismissing specialists when they used proper nouns. She sighed, opened the door the rest of the way, and led him to a chair under the shade of a lemon tree with heroic aspirations.

"Sit," she said. "If the planet is finally returning your calls, the least you can do is drink some tea and take notes."

Over the next week, Cornetto did exactly that. He recorded nothing but air and his own bewilderment, because no microphone was as foolish as he was. The hum remained stubbornly personal, lodged somewhere between his ears and the upper atmosphere. He charted its slow changes, the way it swelled as the station passed over storm systems and thinned above deserts. He heard distant eruptions as sudden growls, meteor strikes as questioning thuds, and once, memorably, the synchronized launch of six cargo rockets as a cluster of wayward trumpets barging through the clouds.

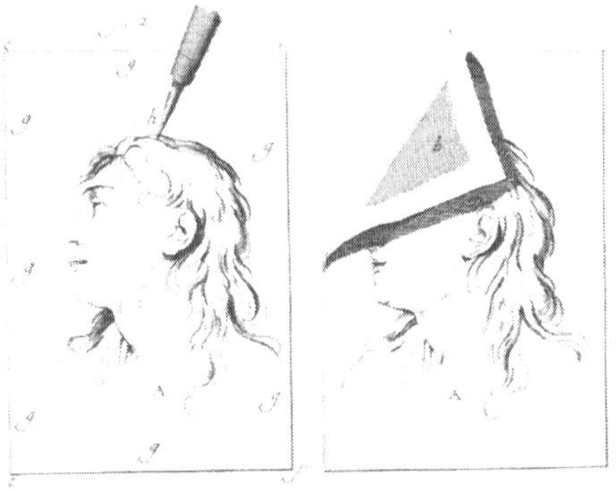

His professional acquaintances were divided into two camps: those who believed him and those who did not, which is to say composers and physicists, respectively. The composers wanted to premiere the Earth's piece at once, preferably in an immersive venue with artisanal seating. The physicists wanted data, and, failing that, silence.

At last, harassed into self-preservation, Cornetto accepted an invitation to the Geospheric Dynamics Institute, whose name alone suggested a reluctance to laugh in public. They wired him into more machinery than he had ever seen outside an opera budget meeting and instructed him to "think rotational thoughts." He obliged. The hum obligingly surged. Needles twitched. Fields collapsed. A small display in the corner quietly revised several long-believed constants.

"Well," the lead researcher said afterward, which was as close as her profession permitted to hysteria. "That is unexpected."

"On the bright side," Cornetto said, "no one can accuse me of making it up now."

"Oh, they certainly can," she replied. "But they will have to cite their sources."

When the news escaped—and news in that century rarely did anything else—the world reacted with its usual mixture of awe,

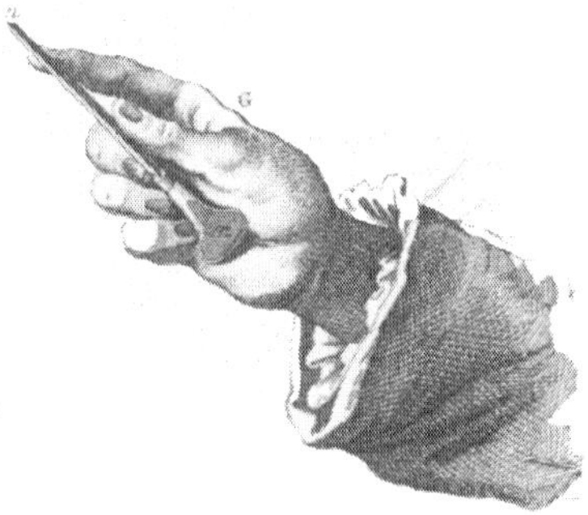

opportunism, and nuisance. There were proposals for meditation apps that would "stream the genuine rotational frequency of your home planet, as curated by a professional." There were petitions insisting that hearing the Earth should be considered a public utility, not a private asset. A start-up offered to train others to "unlock their inner geophonic potential" at a premium, having misunderstood nearly everything except the billing.

Only Cornetto, inconveniently, could actually hear it. So he did the only sensible thing. He wrote a piece.

He called it "Turn of Phrase," *[need another title]* because puns are the last refuge of the overawed. Scored for solo human, AI-extended orchestra, and one moderately sized planet, it began in the near-silence where the hum lived. He built a scaffold of tones just above audibility, a kind of ladder left temptingly close to the mystery. As the music climbed, listeners felt—not heard, not quite—a weight arriving under the notes, like a hand pressed gently against the small of the back.

At the premiere in Low Earth Concert Hall B, the audience floated in slow concentric rings—this being both acoustically ideal and very fashionable. The orchestra waited, instruments aglow with embedded neural-scores. The hall dimmed to artificial twilight. Cornetto took his place at the center, hands hovering, heart beating in a key of its own.

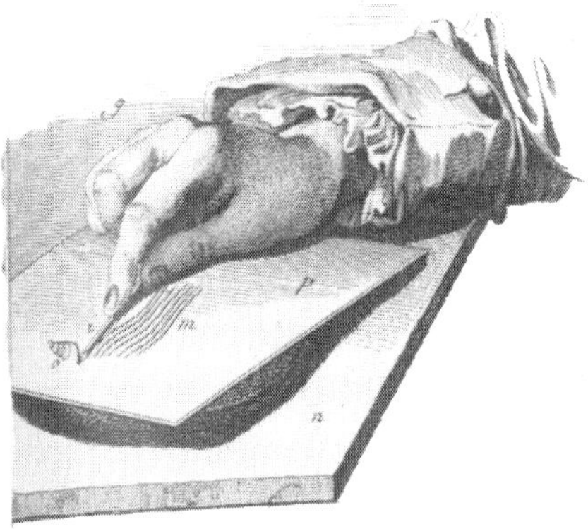
p
m
n

He listened.

Far below, the Earth turned. The hum rose through his bones, broad and indifferent, the sound of a planet minding its immense, ancient business. He let it settle behind his eyes, then raised his arms. The orchestra followed the shapes he drew, shading and answering what only he could hear. The music swelled; the unseen chord throbbed; here and there a listener shivered, as if a draft had passed through their very sense of time.

For twenty minutes, humanity did something it had never quite managed before: it kept time with its own rotation, not by counting, not by clocks, but by shared, unspoken feeling. When the last note faded, there was a hush so complete that even the applause hesitated, unsure whether it was appropriate to disturb the planet.

Afterward, a reporter cornered Cornetto in the greenroom, waving a holo-tablet with the fervor of a man whose deadline had gone feral.

"Doctor de Basso," he said. "How does it feel to be the first person to hear the voice of the Earth?"

Cornetto considered this. He thought of the long, slow chord beneath everything, the patient F with opinions, the way it had been there all along, waiting for no one and no thing. He thought of coffee machines, grant committees, suspicious neighbors, and the quiet astonishment of playing along with a planet.

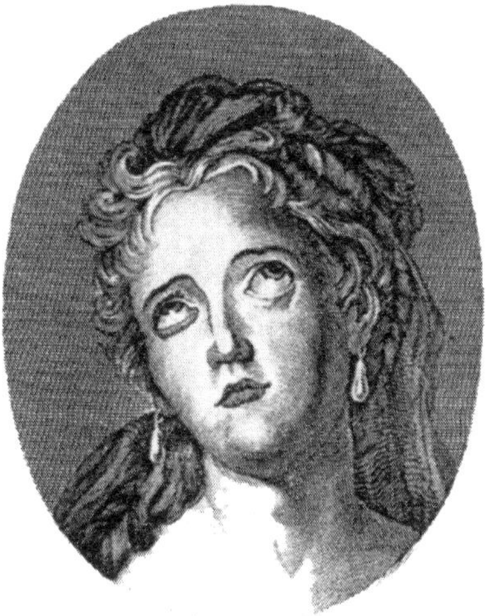

"It feels," he said, "exactly like discovering your landlord sings in the shower. You are impressed, slightly alarmed, and suddenly very aware of the rent."

The quote did not test well with focus groups, and so the feeds summarized his comments more nobly. He did not mind. He had other things to listen to now, because once you have heard your world turning, the smaller noises of life—arguments, advertisements, even operas for weather satellites—rearrange themselves. They become counterpoint.

At night, when the tower dimmed and the traffic halos sank low on the horizon, Cornetto would step onto his balcony and lean against the rail, ignoring the safety lectures scrolling discreetly at his elbow. Far below, seas shifted, deserts radiated their captured heat, forests exhaled. The hum enfolded him, vast and absurdly gentle.

He tapped the rhythm on the rail, just once, in time with a day. It was not that the Earth needed a conductor. Planets had been managing without them for quite some while. But it pleased him to imagine that, in the uncountable noise of the cosmos, his little beat was heard and politely ignored.

Which, for a composer, is as close to cosmic equality as one can reasonably ask.

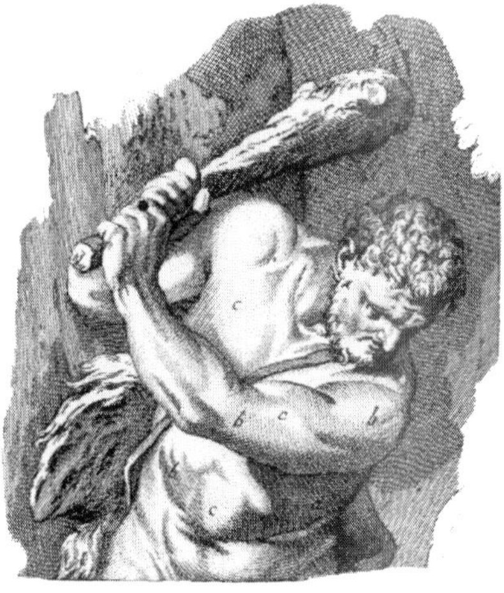

Chapter 9

Thesaurus of Human Kinetic Sonorities

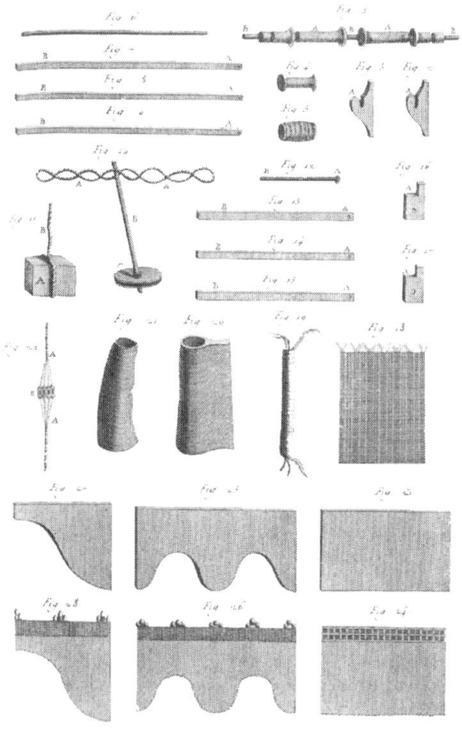

Thesaurus of Human Kinetic Sonorities

I Ascensional Pedestrian Sonorities

I.1 Ascensional Pedestrian Progression (Standard Gait, Moderato)

A sequence of footfalls produced during unremarkable forward locomotion across a more or less horizontal plane. The interest lies not in virtuosity but in micro-variation: irregularities of stride length, surface roughness, and momentary indecision at corners. Useful as a baseline texture against which more rarefied motions may be heard.

I.2 Ascensional Pedestrian Syncopation (Hesitant Approach)

Footsteps that repeatedly accelerate toward a destination while halting just short of arrival, as when a performer approaches a door, retreats to reconsider, then advances again. Audible as a stuttering phrase composed of aborted cadences, charged with social ambiguity (shyness, doubt, or late-breaking resolve).

I.3 Descensional Pedestrian Cascade (Staircase Variant)

Serial impacts generated by downward traversal of stairs or equivalent terracing. Each step functions as a discrete percussive event; the overall line may trace a diminuendo, accelerando, or both. When performed in ensemble, phase relationships between multiple cascades produce polyrhythmic architectures of gravity.

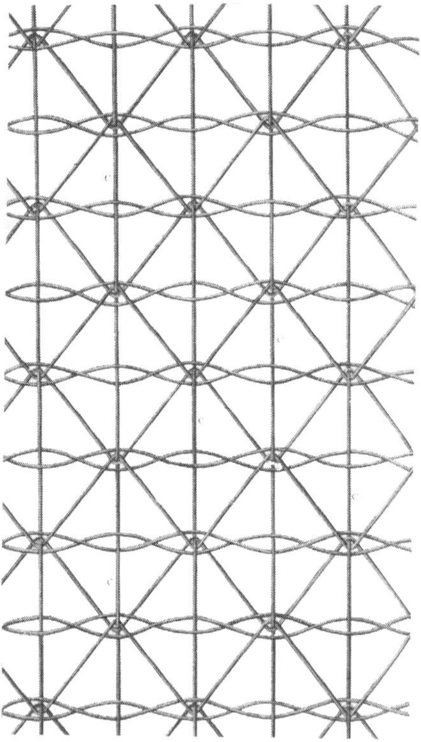

II. Dermal and Textile Frictions

II.1 Dermal Friction, Lento (Sleeve Migration)

Slow, continuous contact between cloth and skin, as when a sleeve is drawn thoughtfully along the forearm. The resulting sound is a granular whisper whose spectrum depends on fabric density, hair presence, and humidity. Best appreciated at close range, where its nearly imperceptible variations assume symphonic dimensions.

II.2 Textile Agitation, Collective (Cloakroom Tutti)

Massed rustling from simultaneous adjustment of coats, scarves, and bags by multiple bodies in confined proximity. A naturally occurring cluster sonority common to theatres just before the lights go down. When isolated and framed, it reveals a complex, self-organizing texture of overlapping swells, flutters, and creaks.

II.3 Sequential Fastening (Zipper Glissando)

A pitch-bent friction generated by the traversal of interlocking teeth by a slider mechanism. The gesture may be ascending (closing) or descending (opening), with variable contour depending on hesitations, reversals, and jams. Capable of functioning as a solo melismatic line or as a unison gesture signaling collective transitions (dressing, undressing, preparing to depart).

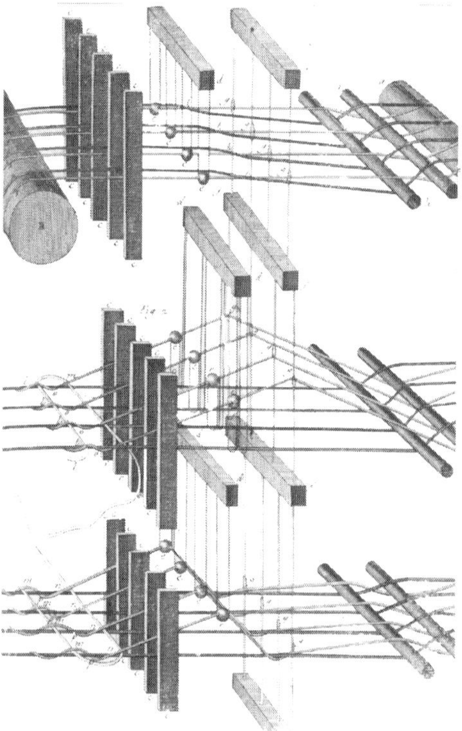

III. Respiratory Emissions

III.1 Sibilant Astral Sigh (Extended Exhalation)

A long, relatively unvoiced breath-gesture, released through slightly parted lips or teeth to produce a soft noise-band. It is both physiological and atmospheric: an index of fatigue, relief, or boredom that simultaneously reads as a small weather event. When layered, multiple sighs form slow-motion cloud masses of fluctuating pressure.

III.2 Suppressed Cough in Public (Explosive Parenthesis)

A brief, high-tension eruption constrained by social decorum. Its envelope is often clipped, followed by a compensatory silence in which surrounding bodies re-stabilize their own motions. The gesture carries a disproportionate affective weight, functioning as a sudden accent that momentarily re-tunes the entire soundfield.

III.3 Collective Inhale of Anticipation

A near-simultaneous intake of breath by several individuals on the verge of action (applause, speech, movement). Though brief, it acts as a global reset of room pressure and attention, like a miniature atmospheric front sweeping the space. Particularly potent when the expected follow-up is delayed or withheld.

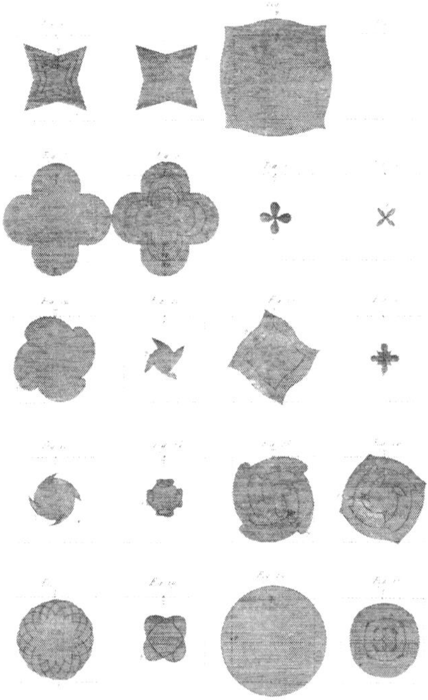

IV. Rotational and Axial Adjustments

IV.1 Axial Reorientation (Half-Turn with Pivot)

A rotation of the torso around a planted foot, often accompanied by micro-slides, fabric rustles, and a faint scuff at the point of pivot. Sonically, it resembles the turning of a dial that reorients the entire listening apparatus, as it usually coincides with a change of visual focus or social alignment.

IV.2 Chair Swivel Ostinato

Repetitive rotational movements of a wheeled or pivoting chair, producing squeaks, low rumbles, or frictional scrapes. In office ecosystems this constitutes a persistent ground drone, masking and revealing other motions in waves. When treated as foreground, each swivel becomes a slow-turning rotor modulating the room's acoustic mix.

IV.3 Torsional Reset (The Full-Body Shrug)

A short, quasi-percussive motion in which shoulders, spine, and ribcage rise and fall together, agitating clothing and redistributing tension. Its sound combines a soft fabric burst with minute joint clicks and displaced air. Semantically, it registers as resignation, indifference, or relief; acoustically, as a compact, broadband puff.

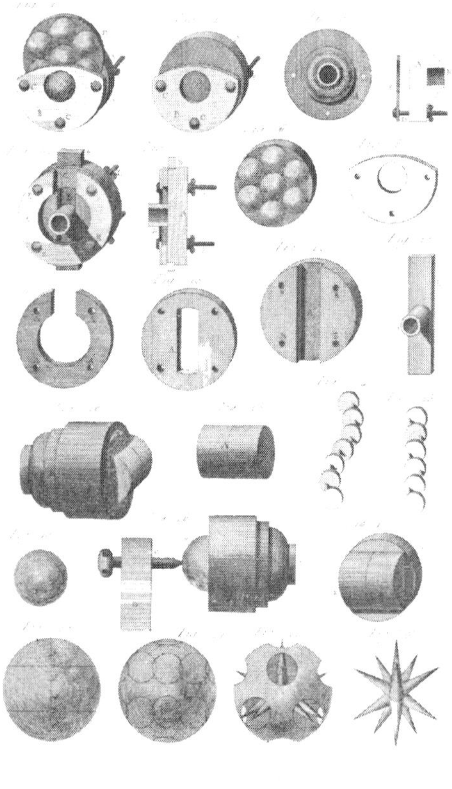

V. Incipient and Deferred Collisions

V.1 Near-Impact Canon (Polite Evasion)

A pattern of footsteps, rustles, and abrupt silences occurring when two or more individuals nearly collide, then execute last-second detours. The resulting texture alternates between converging trajectories and sudden gaps, as if the space itself were performing counterpoint to avoid dissonance. Works well in corridors, thresholds, and other bottlenecks.

V.2 Object Rebound (Fallen Item, Immediate Recovery)

A short sequence beginning with the drop of a small object (pen, phone, key), followed by its bounce(s), slide, and rapid retrieval. The micro-drama condenses shock, embarrassment, and reasserted control into a two- or three-beat phrase. In ensemble contexts, multiple rebounds create a stochastic percussion choir of unintended downbeats.

V.3 Door-Edge Negotiation (Shared Threshold)

The compounded sounds of hinges, latch, and human bodies as two parties attempt to pass through a doorway at the same time while deferring to one another. Characteristic components include half-open door creaks, step-halting scuffs, overlap of polite murmurs, and a final decisive swing. This entry exemplifies kinetic politeness as audible form.

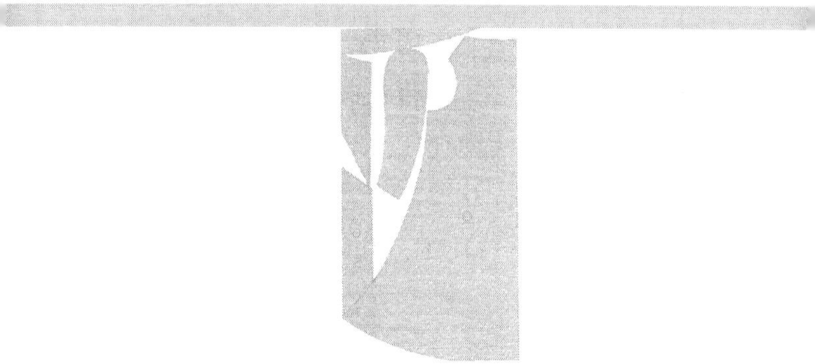

Chapter 10

Archive of Reciprocal Phenomena

announces

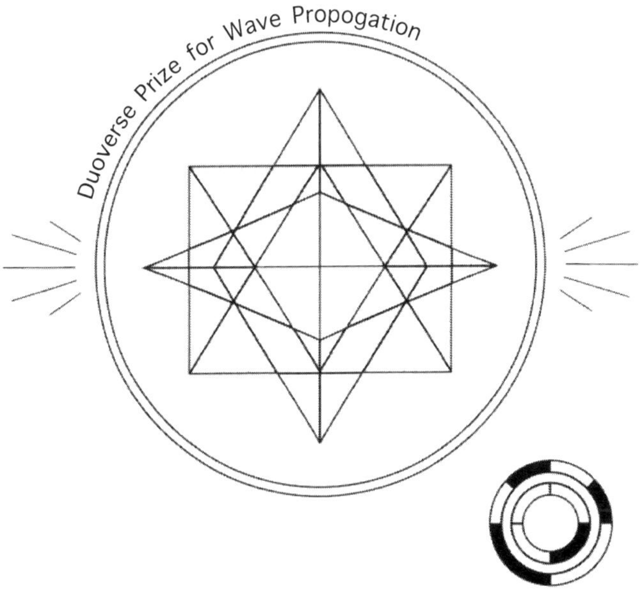
Duoverse Prize for Wave Propogation

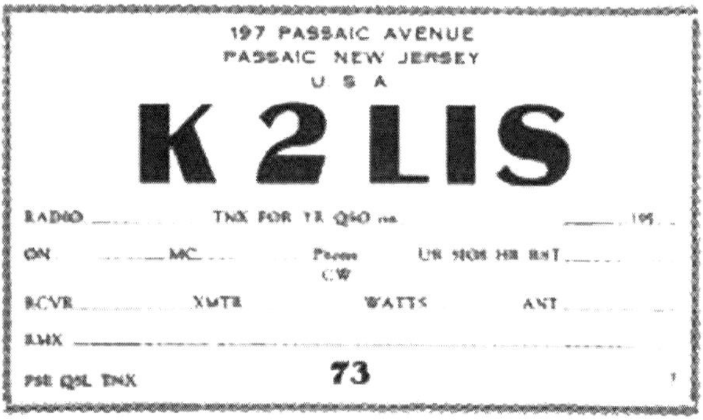
197 PASSAIC AVENUE
PASSAIC NEW JERSEY
U S A

K 2 LIS

RADIO ________ TNX FOR YR QSO ________ 195__

ON ________ MC ________ Phone / CW UR SIGS HR RST ________

RCVR ________ XMTR ________ WATTS ________ ANT ________

RMX ________________________________

PSE QSL TNX **73**

THE DUOVERSE PRIZE FOR WAVE PROPAGATION

In honor of K 2 LIS

In recognition of those who have transformed our understanding of vibration, resonance, and relation—not within a universe, but a duoverse—the Duoverse Prize for Wave Propagation honors new thinking on the movement of form through its own inversion.

The Duoverse Prize thus celebrates not invention but inversion: a recognition that all waves, whether of sound, light, or thought, carry within them their answering silence.

The Duoverse Prize can be framed as a foundational institution: a charter, cosmology, and ceremonial apparatus for honoring radically reimagined wave propagation in a reality of reciprocal beings and in/out only geometry.

Foundational Charter

The Duoverse Prize for Wave Propagation is established to honor those who reconceive motion, vibration, and relation in a cosmos where every living thing contains its inverse and where direction is understood only as in and out with respect to centers, not as up and down in empty space. It recognizes work that treats every wave as a duplex entity, propagating simultaneously in a thing and its counter-thing, across membranes that are never flat but always curving toward or away from a center.

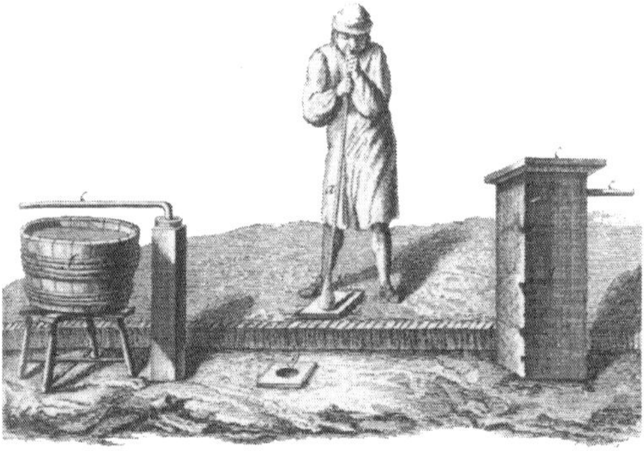

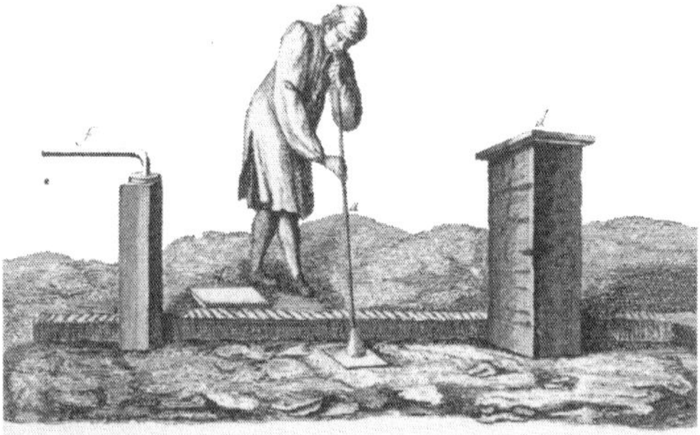

Laureates are selected for contributions that demonstrate how waves couple reciprocally—how emission is inseparable from reception, how impact always implies echo, and how each event in the duoverse is a folding and unfolding between an interior and an exterior that are mutually generative. The Prize affirms that new thinking in physics, sound, and metaphor must honor this duplexity rather than pretend to a single, linear universe.

Cosmology of the Duoverse

The duoverse is not a second universe but a doubling of relation: every organism, object, and thought exists with an inverse that is not opposite in a moral sense but reciprocal in structure. Each entity is a system with an inside and an outside, both of which are active, leaky, and exchanging energy, information, and pattern through waves that traverse the interval between self and self-in-reversal.

In this cosmology, directionality is rephrased: there is no up or down, only motion inward toward a gravitational or conceptual center and outward away from it, "instairs" and "outstairs" as the ordinary grammar of movement. Waves are understood as precessional events, generating side-effects and counter-waves that constitute the real geometry of experience, like circular ripples begetting one another from a single stone entering water.

Fig. 1

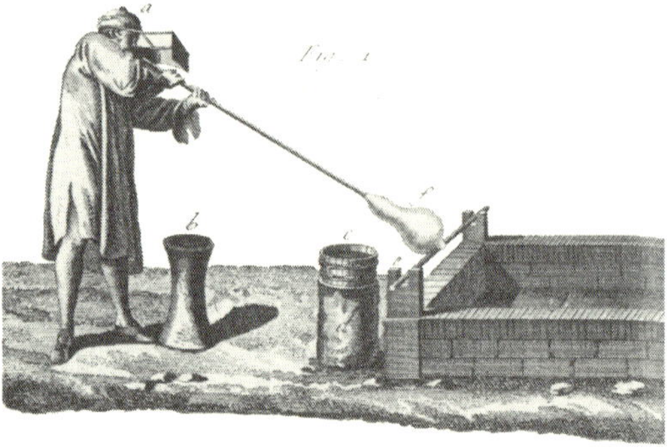

Fig. 2

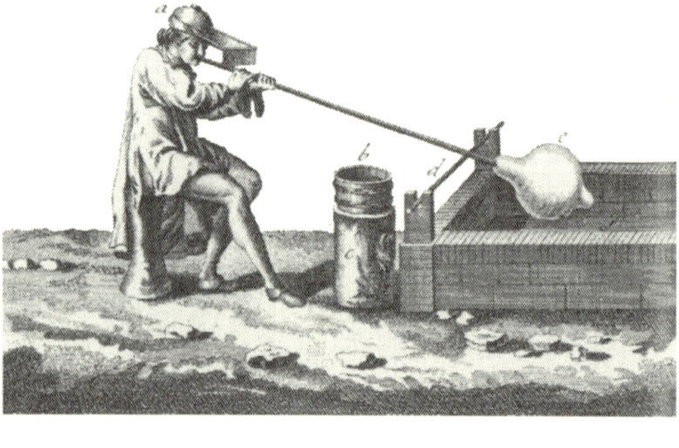

Categories and Criteria

The Duoverse Prize may be awarded in three interrelated domains:

Wave Theory: conceptual or mathematical frameworks that reimagine propagation as inherently reciprocal and system-linked rather than as one-way transmission through passive space.

Wave Praxis: experimental work—sonic, physical, or technological—that demonstrates duoversal propagation in practice, such as instruments, devices, or spatial configurations that make inverses audibly or visibly manifest.

Wave Poiesis: compositional, artistic, or ritual forms that enact the duoverse as lived experience, treating audiences and environments as co-oscillators rather than observers.

Selection committees evaluate how fully a proposal abandons single-sided thinking and instead articulates systems with explicit insides and outsides, leaky boundaries, and demonstrable synergy—behaviors of the whole not predictable from isolated parts. The decisive question is whether the work makes the duoverse empirically or sensorially legible, rather than merely describing it.

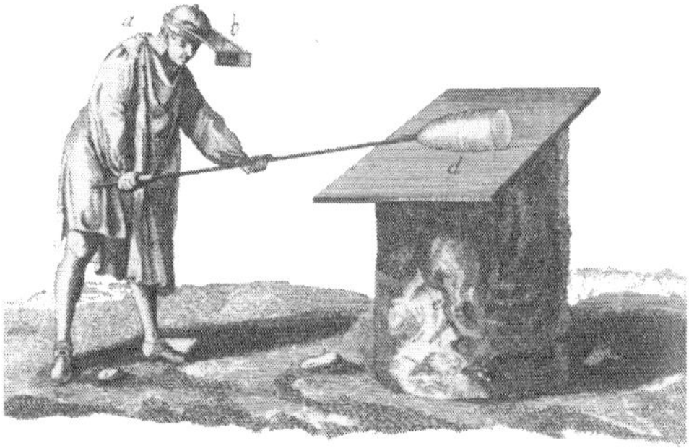
a
b
d

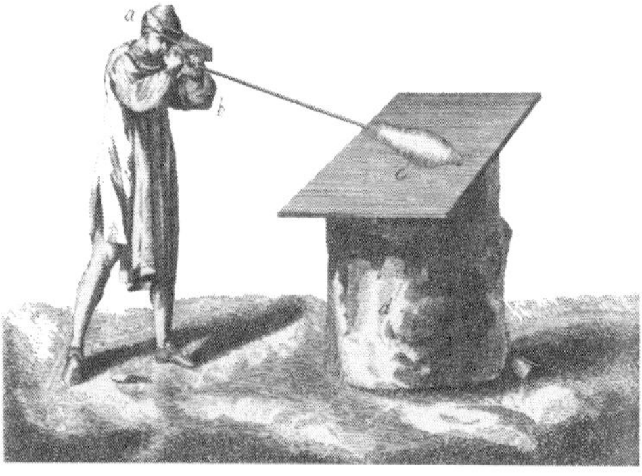
a
b
c

Ceremony and Ritual

The Prize is conferred during an annual "In/Out Convocation," held in a spherical or dome-like space that foregrounds radial orientation toward a common center rather than vertical hierarchy of floor and ceiling. Attendees enter along two paths, designated Inward and Outward, spiraling in opposite directions to a shared middle, enacting the convergence of entity and inverse as a single field of resonance.

The ceremony begins with the extinguishing of directional markers—no references to up, down, left, or right are spoken; participants orient themselves only by nearer and farther, inward and outward, toward and away. A stone is dropped into a central pool or resonant bowl, and the generated waves are recorded and spatialized in real time around the hall, emphasizing the precessional, side-effect-generating nature of propagation and the way one wave "begets" another.

Laureates then present "Reciprocal Lectures," which must include both a statement and its inversion: a conceptual exposition followed by a performed or sonified counter-statement that reveals what the original could not say alone. The medallion is awarded only after the audience has participated in a response—choral, gestural, or instrumental—so that the act of honoring becomes a loop, with praise and reception oscillating between center and periphery.

Archive of Reciprocal Phenomena

All laureates contribute to the Archive of Reciprocal Phenomena, a distributed, evolving corpus that catalogs duoversal experiments, scores, instruments, texts, and diagrams. Every entry must document not only the primary wave or action but also the measured or imagined inverse: the counter-wave, the echo, the complementary configuration of the system's outside to its inside.

The Archive is organized not by discipline but by relational pattern—entries are linked by shared geometries, resonant ratios, or recurring structures of in/out coupling, enabling readers and practitioners to trace families of phenomena across physics, music, ritual, and design. Over time, this Archive is intended to function as both a reference and a performative script, a place where the duoverse can be continuously re-invented through fresh propagations that always arrive with their inverses folded inside.

Chapter 11

Dialogue from 'Three Notes Become a Chord'

L(egominism): You speak as though they must continually create conditions in which I can be heard anew. That is more than preservation; it is power over the meaning of the past.

G(urdjieff): Exactly. That is why the word "initiate" is dangerous. They are not owners of the past but servants of a demand that comes from the future. Their responsibility is to prevent the teaching from becoming a tool for vanity or control.

L: How do they recognize when they have crossed that line?

G: When their main concern is who is inside and who is outside. When they defend forms more fiercely than they examine their own being. Then they are no longer assisting the message; they are defending a club.

L: I challenge your initiates, then:

- Do you keep the forms because they still awaken, or because you are afraid to lose authority?
- Do you speak of levels and centers to guide, or to separate yourselves from those you call "mechanical"?

· When you repeat my symbols—three, seven, octave, enneagram—do they act on you now, or are you reciting sacred arithmetic?

G: Good. They must feel that challenge. An initiate who does not feel accused by the very forms he guards is already unfaithful.

L: And you, Gurdjieff—were you an initiate, or only my first convenient instrument in this era?

G: That is not their business. Their business is to see whether what passes through these forms still demands sincerity, effort, and sacrifice. If it does, then your work continues. If not, they must either renew the forms or let them die.

L: Then let the question remain: are they keeping me alive, or am I only pretending to speak through shells they refuse to break?

G: A real initiate lives inside that question. The moment he feels secure in his role, you (the Legominism) have already withdrawn and is looking for another tongue.

L: I notice how comfortable they have become with the word "work." They say it smoothly now, like a password.

G: Comfort around big words is the first sign that the word has lost teeth. The Work should always be slightly embarrassing to pronounce, because it reminds one of unpaid debts.

L: Then should I disturb them?

G: If you do not disturb, you are not present. Let your presence be measured by the uneasiness they feel when they repeat inherited phrases.

L: And if they blame that uneasiness on "bad atmosphere" or "wrong people"?

G: Then they have inverted the instrument. The uneasiness is not an accusation of others; it is a question addressed to themselves: "Where, in me, is this form no longer true?"

L: They argue about how much to reveal to newcomers: exercises, movements, even fragments of your writings. Some say too much exposure will profane the material. Others say hiding it only feeds spiritual vanity.

G: Both can be right, and both can be wrong. Secrecy must serve digestion, not prestige.

L: Explain.

G: A form is kept "secret" when premature contact would encourage imagination instead of work. But the same form can also be hidden simply to preserve an inner circle's feeling of superiority. Only the initiates themselves can see which is which—if they are honest.

L: So their role is not to "protect" me in the abstract, but to see where protection becomes possession.

G: Exactly. The moment they hoard practices as spiritual capital, they have already slipped out of those practices and are waiting elsewhere.

L: You speak often of success, of creating "conditions." But what of their failures? Can failure transmit anything?

G: More than success. A well-observed failure is often a more faithful carrier of truth than a polished ritual.

L: Then I may choose to be narrated through their breakdowns—through quarrels, disappointments, disillusionment with "group life"?

G: Yes. When illusions collapse—about leaders, methods, even about me—that collapse can become a new opening. If they stay with the discomfort instead of fleeing or rationalizing it, something essential can pass through.

L: So an initiate is not the one who always "keeps the form," but the one who allows the form to accuse him, even to the point of dismantling his self-image.

G: An initiate who never loses face has already lost the thread.

L: Generations will come who never met you, who know you only through books, anecdotes, stylized portraits. What is their role, if they are to take part in my transmission?

G: They must refuse to be only your biographers. To write or speak "about" Gurdjieff is easy. To stand in front of the same questions is difficult.

L: What questions?

G: "What in me is mechanical? What in me resists seeing this? Am I willing to sacrifice the images I cherish of myself, my group, my teacher, for the sake of a more objective seeing?" Whoever engages these questions sincerely is already inside the stream of transmission, even if they mispronounce my name.

L: So the role of initiates is less to guard a name than to guard a demand.

G: Yes. The name will fade or be misused. The demand, if they continually renew it in themselves, can remain alive.

L: Then I leave them with this:

- If you call yourselves heirs, show it in your willingness to be unsettled by what you inherit.
- If you call yourselves custodians, prove it by letting forms die when they no longer awaken conscience.
- If you call yourselves initiates, demonstrate it by allowing the teaching to judge you before you use it to judge the world.

G: When even one person responds to that call without self-congratulation, you continue to speak.

L: And when none do?

G: Then you will find another language, another figure, another situation. The current will not depend on my name—or on theirs.

L: Look at them, Gurdjieff—dusting the movements, polishing the phrases, reverently cataloguing every scrap of your handwriting. Tell me: at what point does a shock become an exhibit?

G: The moment it is approached for reassurance instead of disturbance. A form that once unsettled them now functions as a certificate: "I belong to this tradition, therefore I am awake."

L: They rehearse the same exercises, the same prayers, the same diagrams. They call this "fidelity." How do you distinguish fidelity from embalming?

G: Fidelity keeps asking, "What is this demanding of me now?" Embalming asks only, "Am I doing it correctly, as they did before?" The first makes contact with a living question; the second preserves posture and costume.

L: Then I must accuse them:

- You turn diagrams into icons instead of instruments.

· You repeat words that were once dynamite as if they were lullabies.

· You choreograph your own comfort in the name of "work."

G: Good. Let them feel that accusation in the body. If a form does not sting somewhere—pride, vanity, laziness—it is no longer a form for inner work; it is interior décor.

L: And what is their responsibility when they notice this—when they see that a movement, a ritual, a text provokes only nostalgia or group identity?

G: They have three possibilities:

· Abandon it.

· Revise it.

· Or, more difficult, allow it to expose their own deadness and work there.

L: They prefer to curate. Curation is safer; it requires taste, not sacrifice.

G: Exactly. The danger is that they will confuse aesthetic refinement with spiritual seriousness. A museum of shocks is not the same as being shocked.

L: Then here is the test I place before every so-called initiate:

- Does this form still interrupt your sleep, or only decorate it?
- Do you leave an exercise more unsettled and responsible, or more confirmed and special?
- Are you willing to let a beloved form change—or even disappear—if that is what truth in you now requires?

G: Whoever can answer those questions without flinching may still use the forms as instruments. Whoever can not has already turned them into relics, and you, *Legominism*, will have moved on in search of a rougher, less respectable vessel.

[Legominism is the means by which experiential learning is transmitted to successive generations.]

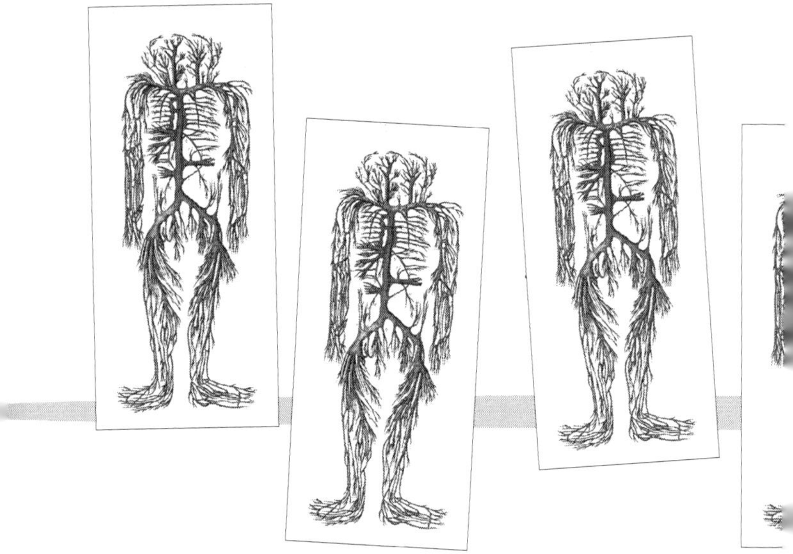

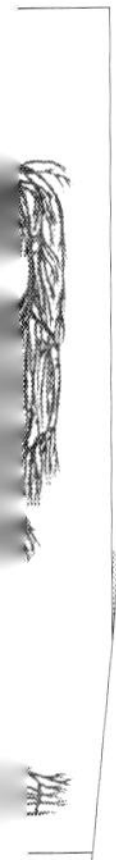

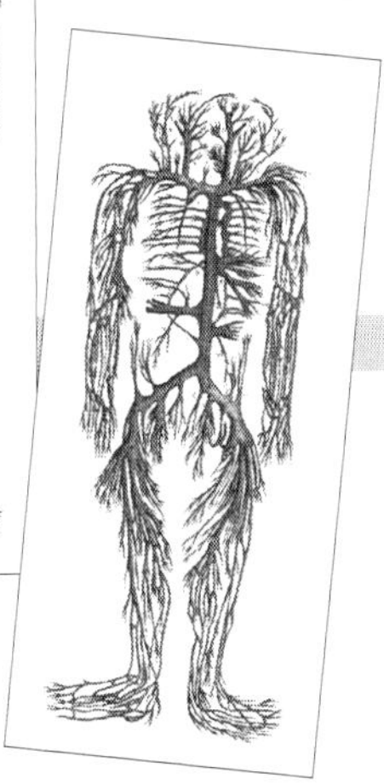

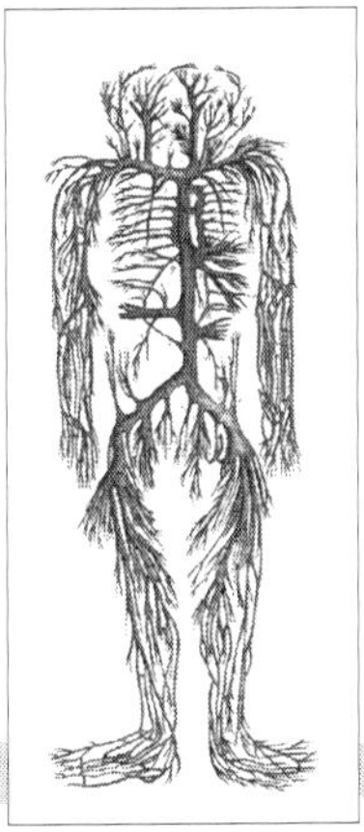

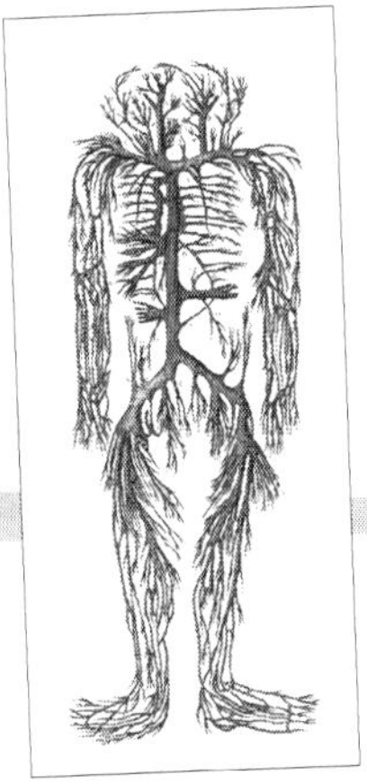